The Water Babies

A Play

Willis Hall

With songs by
John Cooper

Based on the story by
Charles Kingsley

Samuel French – London
New York – Sydney – Toronto – Hollywood

ISBN 0 573 08076 3

THE WATER BABIES

First presented at the Arts Centre, Warwick on 3rd February, 1986, and subsequently on a national tour by the Flying Tortoise Theatre Company, with the following cast of characters:

Thomas Grimes, a chimney sweep	Trevor Peake
Potman	Christopher Preston
Tom, a chimney-sweep's apprentice	Helen Copp
Irishwoman	Janet Behan
Burrell, a gamekeeper	Christopher Preston
Sir John Harthover	Gil Sutherland
Pritchard, a housemaid	Helen Sheals
Ellie Harthover, Sir John's daughter	Dorcas Morgan
Nurse	Linda Rusby
Gardener	Peter Stone
Old Woman	Linda Rusby
Male Water-Otter	Gil Sutherland
Female Water-Otter	Linda Rusby
Lobster	Trevor Peake
Doctor	Christopher Preston
Mrs Bedonebyasyoudid	Janet Behan
Mrs Doasyouwouldbedoneby	Janet Behan
1st Prison Warder	Gil Sutherland
2nd Prison Warder	Christopher Preston

Directed by Ian Watt-Smith
Designed by Alexander McPherson
Musical Director Tam Neal

CHARACTERS

Thomas Grimes, a chimney-sweep
Potman
Tom, a chimney-sweep's apprentice
Irishwoman
Burrell, a gamekeeper
Sir John Harthover
Pritchard, a housemaid
Ellie Harthover, Sir John's daughter
Nurse
Gardener
Old Woman
Male Water-Otter
Female Water-Otter
Lobster
Doctor
Mrs Bedonebyasyoudid
Mrs Doasyouwouldbedoneby
1st Prison Warder
2nd Prison Warder
Water Babies
Fishes
Villagers

MUSICAL NUMBERS

ACT I

1	**When All The World Is Young, Lad**	Company
2	**Excuses, Excuses!—Long Hard Road**	Grimes and Tom
2a	**Long Hard Road** (Reprise)	Grimes and Tom
3	**Never Seen Anything**	Company
3a	**Never Seen Anything** (reprise)	Housemaid
3b	**Never Seen Anything** (reprise)	Tom
4	**Stop That Lad**	Company
5	**Come With Me**	Irishwoman
6	**I'm Clean**	Tom and Otters

ACT II

7	**Welcome Tom** (reprise of Song 5)	Irishwoman
8	**Down To The Sea**	Company
9	**There's Always an Answer**	Lobster and Tom
10	**The Other-End-of-Nowhere**	Tom and Irishwoman
11	**There's Always An Answer** (reprise)	Mrs Bedonebyasyoudid and Lobster
12	**Go To Sleep**	Water Babies
13	**The Other-End-of-Nowhere** (reprise)	Tom and Ellie
14	**Excuses, Excuses** (reprise)	Grimes and Warder
15	**Finale**	Company

The piano/vocal score is available on sale from Samuel French Ltd

SYNOPSIS OF SCENES

ACT I

SCENE 1 The Drum and Monkey Inn
SCENE 2 On the Road
SCENE 3 Harthover Park
SCENE 4 Harthover Hall
SCENE 5 Ellie's Bedroom
SCENE 6 The Cottage by the River
SCENE 7 A Country Churchyard
SCENE 8 The River-Bed

ACT II

SCENE 1 The River-Bed
SCENE 2 The Edge of the Sea
SCENE 3 Harthover Hall
SCENE 4 Under the Sea
SCENE 5 The Journey
SCENE 6 The Other-End-of-Nowhere
SCENE 7 Back on Dry Land

PRODUCTION NOTE

In the original professional touring production of this play, the Water Babies and the Fishes were represented by puppets. These puppets were controlled by puppeteers, dressed all in black, working in ultra-violet lighting and therefore invisible to the audience.

But each society contemplating tackling this piece may care to consider devising ways of overcoming the problem of depicting the underwater life. Schools' productions, for example, could use small children to play both the Water Babies and the Fishes.

Again in the touring production, the cast was limited to nine actors and actresses who, in some cases, not only had to double several roles but also had to leap in and out of puppeteers' costumes.

Amateur societies, of course, will not usually be limited by a lack of numbers. They should not only be able to fill each separate role but might even consider adding to the cast-list by creating some non-speaking parts—more members of the squire's household staff, for instance, or more undersea creatures.

In short, each producer should see the script as a starting-out point to be built upon or cut down to size, depending upon his or her society's resources.

Willis Hall

ACT I

SCENE 1

The Drum and Monkey Inn

We are outside a village inn and our setting need be no more than a rough-hewn table and bench and, perhaps, an inn-sign

We open on a pastoral Victorian scene in which as many members of the cast as we may muster, dressed as Villagers, are "frozen" on stage as the CURTAIN *rises or the Lights come up. They "come to life" as the opening music comes in behind and they sing*

Song 1: When All the World is Young, Lad

Company When all the world is young, lad
And all the trees are green
And every goose a swan, lad
And every lass a queen
Then hey for boot and horse, lad
And round the world away
Young blood must have its course, lad
And every dog its day.

There follows a short dance to the above tune and the number concludes with the company repeating the last four lines of the verse

At the end of the song, the Villagers go off about their various business

Mr Grimes, the chimney-sweep, is left sitting at the table cradling a tankard and smoking a clay pipe

The Potman enters and crosses with a full tankard of ale and changes it for Grimes's empty one

Grimes takes a swig at the new tankard, belches loudly, then cocks an aggrieved eye at the Potman

Grimes Well?
Potman My master says to tell you there's tuppence to pay.

Grimes digests this information, belches again, takes another swig at his ale and then looks the Potman up and down

Grimes What else has your master told you to tell me?
Potman Nothing else, Mr Grimes.

Grimes Have you not got work to do? Are there not pots to wash and pans to scrub and floors to be kept tidy?

Potman My master told me to wait for the money.

Grimes Are you telling me my name's no good here any longer?

Potman No, Mr Grimes. Not me, Mr Grimes.

Grimes You'd better not—or else there will be bother! You've heard of Sir John Harthover who lives at Harthover Hall, no less?

Potman Who hasn't?

Grimes You'll be telling me next that Sir John's name is no good here either?

Potman I wouldn't!

Grimes You would put the cat among the wood-pigeons then! Sir John and me are old acquaintances of many years standing. Very old acquaintances. There's many and many a time I've faced Sir John across the public court. Him on the magistrates' bench and me in the dock. "Fourteen days, Grimes!" "Very good, Sir John. God bless you!" I call him Sir John and he calls me Grimes, there's no standing on ceremony between us. Look down that road.

The Potman peers along the road

What do you see?

Potman Not a lot.

Grimes Tell me.

Potman An old Irishwoman in a grey shawl sitting by the roadside with her belongings in a bundle.

Grimes Your eyesight does you credit—how do you know she's Irish?

Potman I've seen her before.

Grimes You don't see a boy pushing a cart?

Potman No, Mr Grimes.

Grimes A cart that's loaded with chimney-sweep's brushes and pushed by a little thin white-faced lad—leastways, he would be a white-faced lad if you were ever to wash him, God forbid. That lad will rue the day that he was whelped. Now then, you may go inside and tell your master that, when my lad turns up, and after I've knocked him to the ground, he shall be pushing my cart to Harthover Hall. Tell your master I am hired by Sir John Harthover to sweep his chimbleys. Tell him he'll be paid in full, this evening.

Potman Yes, Mr Grimes.

Grimes gives the Potman his empty tankard

Grimes And get that filled and quick about it. (*He takes a grubby spotted handkerchief out of his pocket and hands that also to the Potman*) Here—and put me a slice of bread and a hunk of cheese in that. It's a long hard hike to Harthover Hall and uphill mostly. I shall need to pause on the way for a bite.

The Potman moves to leave, glancing along the road again

Potman I think your lad's coming now, Mr Grimes.

The Potman goes off

Tom enters, pushing the hand-cart which is full of Grimes's brushes and equipment. Tom is black from head to foot and should be around eleven years old

Grimes Tom.
Tom Yes, master?
Grimes Come thee here and stand before me.

Tom does so, cowering with fear, aware of what is to come. Grimes cuffs Tom's head, knocking him to the ground

Get up. Do you know what that was for?
Tom No, master.
Grimes (*cuffing him again*) Don't answer back. You're late.

Over the following, the Potman returns with Grimes's tankard and his bread and cheese

Grimes downs the tankard of ale in one gulp and slips the bread and cheese into his pocket

You were sent to fetch that cart from outside the *Nag's Head* an hour ago.
Tom The landlord wouldn't let me take it, master. He said you owe him money still for ale you've supped. I had to wait until his back was turned afore I could run off with it.

Grimes cuffs Tom again

SONG 2: Excuses, Excuses!—Long Hard Road

Grimes Excuses, excuses
All the time excuses
Is it your intention to lie idling all the day?
Excuses, excuses
All the time excuses
Get thissen be'ind that cart and let's be on our way.
Tom But Mr Grimes, sir, it seems that every time, sir,
When I try to please you I cannot appease you.
Grimes To your task, boy and get up off that grass, boy
Before I pick you up myself and kick you up the——
Tom (*getting up smartly*) Nasty!
Grimes No more excuses, no more lazy ruses
We must be at Harthover by noon to do the job.You must move nimbly—there's a dozen chimbleys
To climb and clean and sweep before we earn a bob.
And once we're there don't let me catch you talking to the nobs.

Tom takes hold of the cart and falls in behind Grimes who sets out at a brisk pace for Harthover Hall. Tom struggles to keep up. The Lights fade as Tom and Grimes move on, with the music held behind. The Lights come up again on:

Scene 2

On the Road

There should be some suggestion of bleak moorland. There is a low dry-stone wall and a milestone on which is inscribed: "HARTHOVER—2 miles"

Tom is still pushing the cart and following Grimes, as:

Song 2 (*continued*)

Tom It's a long hard road
Grimes Excuses
Tom And the way is never ending
Grimes Always excuses
Tom Bending round the hills and moorland
Grimes Push you little toad
Tom When I'm getting tired
Grimes Faster! Remember who's the master
Tom Wonder how it would be
If ever I was free
Of this heavy load
It's a long hard road
Grimes It's a long hard road
Both It's a long hard road

Grimes looks over his shoulder impatiently at Tom

Grimes Push, lad, push! Put your back into it!
Tom Can we not rest awhile, master?
Grimes I wish we could lad—and had I nobbut meself to think about, we would. But I have you to consider. You're a right burden to me, Tom. If we stop now, you'll be going up them chimbleys after nightfall—with never so much as a crack of light to see where you're going, and where would you be then?
Tom In the dark, Mr Grimes.

Grimes, who has paused to wipe the sweat from his brow and waited for Tom to catch up with him, cuffs the lad again

Grimes Don't be cheeky. (*He spots the milestone*) There, you see—only two more miles to go.
Tom Is it uphill all the way?
Grimes What if it is? Think of the joy and pleasure you'll derive coming back. Perhaps we will just rest our legs for a minute, that ale I supped is fetching out a rare sweat on me.

Grimes sits on the dry-stone wall and takes out his handkerchief-wrapped bread and cheese. Tom leans against the cart

The Irishwoman enters, carrying her bundle of belongings. She is a "tall handsome woman with heavy black hair hanging about her cheeks". She has a grey shawl over her head and a crimson petticoat, but has neither shoes nor stockings

Grimes studies the Irishwoman as she approaches them

This is a hard road, mother, for a body without shoes on her feet. Will you wait awhile and take a ride on the cart?

Irishwoman That's a fine offer indeed, but who would be the workhorse, tell me?

Grimes Why, the lad of course—who else is there?

The Irishwoman looks Tom up and down and shakes her head

Irishwoman No, thank you kindly, Mr Grimes—I'll not be needing the ride. But I will bide a while and exchange a word with the boy, if you've no objections.

Grimes You may please yourself.

Grimes eats his bread and cheese. The Irishwoman sits on the milestone

Irishwoman Where do you come from? Where do you live?

Tom I sleep under the stairs in my master's house.

Irishwoman Under the stairs? Do you own nothing of your own then?

Tom All that I stand up in. And three marbles and a button with a bit of string on it. (*He takes these out of his pocket and shows them to her*)

Irishwoman Where are your parents then?

Tom Dead. Mr Grimes took me from the workhouse for his apprentice.

Irishwoman And what would you like to do, child, when you grow up?

Tom I want to be like Mr Grimes, of course. I want to own my own brushes and my own cart and my own apprentice too, to knock to the ground and send up chimneys.

The Irishwoman "tut-tuts" and shakes her head, then:

Irishwoman Do you say your prayers at night?

Tom No, missis. I don't know any prayers to say. Where do you live, missis?

Irishwoman Far away. By the sea.

Tom The sea! I've never seen the sea—but I heard tell of it. What's the sea like, missis?

Irishwoman Cruel and kind. Cruel when it roars and rages over the rocks on stormy winter's nights. Kind when it lies still and quiet on summer days for little children to bathe and play in.

Tom I wish, one day, that I could run down into the sea.

Grimes, who has been eavesdropping, gives a coarse laugh

Grimes You! A sweep's lad? What need do you have to go getting water splashed all over you? You'd only get yourself all mucky again the next time you went up a chimbley. Take yourself into the sea indeed! Whoever heard the like! (*He has finished his bread-and-cheese. He lifts himself over the wall and splashes water on to his face from a moorside stream*)

Tom What are you doing, master?

Grimes Swilling my face, of course, in this here stream—what does it look as if I'm doing?

Tom Why, master, I never saw you do that before!

Grimes Nor will again, most likely. (*He now uses the handkerchief as a towel*) I wasn't dirty, don't go thinking that. T'wasn't for cleanliness I did it, but for coolness. I'd be ashamed to want washing every week or so, like any smutty collier-lad.

Tom I wish I might go and dip my head in that stream. It must feel as good as putting it under the town pump—and there is no beadle here to drive a lad away.

Grimes clambers back over the dry-stone wall

Grimes Washing yourself now, is it? Lah-de-dah! Bathing yersen one minute and washing your face the next! Airs and graces. What do you want with washing yersen? There's no tankards-full of ale in your belly, is there, bringing out a sweat?

Tom I am hot though, master. If you can swill your face, why can't I?

Grimes Because I says not.

Tom I've as much right to swill my face as you have yours—it's not your stream.

Tom marches towards the stream in a sudden show of defiance, but Grimes grabs hold of him

Grimes No, and neither is it yours, lad. But you belong to me, and well you know it! (*He cuffs Tom to the ground again*) And if I tell you "nay", you shall not!

Tom is hurt more than before and he sobs quietly to himself as he picks himself up

Irishwoman Are you not ashamed of yourself, Thomas Grimes.

Grimes No—nor ever was yet.

Irishwoman True for you. If you ever had been ashamed of yourself you would have gone over into Vendale long ago.

Grimes What do you know about Vendale?

Irishwoman I know about Vendale, and about you too. I know, for instance, what happened in Aldermire Copse, by night, two years ago come Martinmas.

Grimes *You* do?

Irishwoman Yes, I was there.

Grimes By God, missis, you know more than your share for an Irish tinker woman on the road—if Irish tinker woman thou art—which I'm beginning very much to doubt! And if tinker woman thou art not—in hell's name, who are you?

Irishwoman Never mind who I am. I saw what I saw. I know what I know. And if you ever strike that boy again, I shall tell every word of it.

Grimes (*glowering at the Irishwoman, puzzled, angry and a little afraid, then turning to Tom*) It's time you and I were on our way, lad. Our business lies with the chimbleys of a high-born gentleman—not with some old biddy on the moors. Pick up that cart, Tom.

Tom takes hold of the cart-shafts and Grimes turns his back on the Irishwoman

Irishwoman Stop! I have one more word for you both—for both of you will see me again before all is over. Those that wish to be clean, clean they will be—and those that wish to be foul, foul they will be. Remember that.

With which, she slips over the dry-stone wall and is gone

Grimes hesitates a moment and then crosses to the wall, calling after her

Grimes You come back here, missis! I haven't finished with you yet either—(*But, to his surprise, he discovers that the Irishwoman is nowhere in sight*) Where's she gone? Where's she disappeared to?

The sun has disappeared too and a chill wind begins to strike across the moors

Miles and miles of empty moorland and not so much as a sight of her. And why is it turned chill so much of a sudden? (*He pulls his collar up around his ears as he calls across the moors again*) And another thing, who told you my name was Thomas Grimes? Who told you my name was Thomas Grimes, missis! I'm not afraid of you! I'm not!

But there is no answer—and the wind is growing stronger as it whistles across the moors. Grimes turns back to Tom

Come, lad—don't stand there goggle-eyed. Get your back into your work and give that cart some pasty—or would you sooner feel the back of my hand? (*He raises his hand to strike Tom again but thinks better of it and glances around nervously*) Push, lad, push hard!

Song 2A: Long Hard Road (Reprise)

Tom It's a long hard road
Grimes Don't tell me that I know
Tom And I fear that I'm still weary
Grimes The moor is weird and eerie
Both Suddenly I feel a chill
An ill-wind 'twas that blowed
Suddenly gone cold
Wonder what the future's holding
But I'm going to be bold
Grimes Can't you do as you're told
Just keep pushing that load
Both It's a long hard road
It's a long hard road
It's a long hard road

And they set off again along the moorland path, moving slower now as they head into the wind. Then, as they go off, we go to:

Scene 3

Harthover Park

We are in the grounds of Harthover Hall, which may be represented by a piece of garden statuary; a length of formal decorative wall or, perhaps, a flower-decked gothic urn

As Grimes and Tom have gone off at one side of the stage, Sir John's Gamekeeper, Burrell, enters at the other, followed by Sir John himself who may or may not (depending upon the cast's availability) be attended by a Manservant

Gamekeeper Very good, Sir John—I'll attend to that, you may depend upon it—and I'll take a walk up as far as the top spinney too this morning—for there's somebody been wandering around up there that had no right to.
Sir John More trespassers, Burrell?
Gamekeeper A sight more sinister than trespassers on this occasion.
Sir John Not poachers again?

The Gamekeeper nods

Are you sure of it?

The Gamekeeper pulls a gin-trap out of his game bag

Gamekeeper That I am—they left their calling-card. And speaking of poachers, Sir John—here's someone now that I wouldn't trust within a mile of a rabbit hole . . .

Over which, Grimes has entered followed by Tom who is still pushing the cart

That'll do, Grimes—you just hold hard and stand your ground until I tells you different.

Grimes and Tom come to a halt. Sir John peers across at Grimes, curious

Sir John Don't I know you, fellow?
Grimes You does indeed, Sir John! Good-day to you, gamekeeper! (*Then back to Sir John*) It's Grimes, your honour. Thomas Grimes. We've knowed each other across the public court on any one of a dozen meetings. Why, there's many and many a time you've given me fourteen days, in your infinite wisdom, and delighted I've been to do my dooty and serve your sentence.
Sir John Are you a poacher?
Gamekeeper And worse.
Grimes No, your honour—I'm a chimbley-sweep. And here's my cart and brushes and apprentice-lad too to prove it. Touch your head to his honour, Tom.

Sir John And what have I had cause to send you down for?

Grimes Ah! What haven't you had cause to send me down for might be an easier question. Drunkenness, as often as not—drunkenness and subsequent misdemeanours aggravated by the drink; fisticuffs; damage to private property—but nothing of any great importance, as I'm sure you'll allow. Generally, your honour, for being as drunk as a magistrate—no offence intended. But today, Sir John, I stands in front of you as sober as the day is long—well, almost—and come about honest, lawful business. I'm here to sweep your chimbleys—which is what I'll get about doing and not detain your honour any longer, as I knows we're both of us busy men. Come on, Tom.

Gamekeeper No, you don't—you'll do as I say, Thomas Grimes, and not move from that spot until I'm good and ready to go with you.

Sir John But you can't go with him Burrell—you're needed at the trout-stream—and you've the top spinney poachers to take care of.

Gamekeeper I'd sooner put my trust in poachers, Sir John, than allow Grimes to wander unattended in the grounds. I *knows* him, sir, of old—and I wouldn't care to consider the mischief he might get up to without an eye kept on him ...

At which point, a Housemaid, Pritchard, enters, running hard, head-down, and not looking where she is going. She is a nervous diminutive girl who does everything at the double. She pulls up short as she almost bumps into Sir John. She bobs him a couple of quick curtsies

Housemaid Oh, sir, beggin' y'r pardin', sir!

Sir John Yes, Pritchard—what is it?

Housemaid Mrs Lewthwaite sent me out, sir, when she spotted the chimbley-sweep in the drive, sir. On'y I've been right round the rosebushes and down as far as the rhododendrons, an' I can't see sight nor sound of 'im, sir, beggin' y'r pardin'!

Sir John directs her attention towards Grimes and the Housemaid turns—and almost jumps out of her skin

Lawks-a-mercy—it's 'im—an' with a lad in tow to match the fire-back!

Song 3: Never Seen Anything

(*Singing*) Oh, I've never seen anything quite so mucky in all my years
Just by standing beside him you have to be plucky

Tom, uncomprehending, moves towards her

Don't touch me—I'll burst into tears
He's totally black from the front to the back
Oh, alas and alack—like a coalman's sack
I've never seen anything quite so mucky in all my years

Gamekeeper I've never seen anything quite so dirty in all my days
From the tip of his toes to the top of his shirt he's

Filthy—kindly avert your gaze!
He must have disease and there's probably fleas
From his head to his knees—someone scrub him please!
I've never seen anything quite so dirty in all my days

Sir John I've never seen anything quite so nasty in all my life
Evil and unbelievably ghastly
Please don't let him go near the wife
She'd faint if she saw
Watch the paint on the door
Cover carpets and floor
Cover him what's more
I've never seen anything quite so nasty in all my life

Trio Here, at Harthover Hall, you see
We live in a world of aristocracy
Our house and our bodies and our minds are clean
And we won't allow anything to come between

Sir John So take him behind
Out of sight, out of mind

Gamekeeper You will probably find
He's the thieving kind

Trio Oh, we've never seen anything quite so nasty

Sir John Filthy

Housemaid Dirty

Gamekeeper Mucky

Trio Ghastly!
Never seen anything quite so nasty in
The days and months and years of our natural lives!

Sir John And now that you have located him Pritchard, what other instructions do you have?

Housemaid (*another quick curtsy, then*) Why, sir, I'm to h'accompany 'im round the back, an' to see to it that 'ee don't go near the front, nor on the terrace, nor finger-mark the paintwork, an' neither clump 'is mucky 'ob-nailed boots on the 'all-tiles what's only just been scrubbed.

Sir John And quite right too. In which circumstance, Burrell, we can leave—er—what's the fellow call himself—— ?

Grimes Grimes, your honour—Thomas Grimes, master chimbley-sweep.

Sir John —leave Grimes in Pritchard's tender care while you and I attend to the trout-stream.

Gamekeeper As you wish, Sir John. (*To the Housemaid*) Only see to it that you don't allow your eyes to stray from off the cunning wretch's carcass for so much as an instant.

The Housemaid bobs the Gamekeeper one of her curtsies

Housemaid Very good, Mr Burrell.

Sir John and the Gamekeeper go off

Grimes (*calling after them*) Good-day to you, Sir John—I shall look forward to the pleasure of your company next time I'm in the dock—and to obliging you by honouring any sentence you might give me. (*He cuffs Tom impatiently*) Touch your head, lad, touch your head! Show some servility!

Over which, the Housemaid has crossed and is peering at Tom with keen interest

Housemaid My stars though! He is a sight for sore eyes, an' no mistake! Did you ever *see* so much muck? He's as black as an old tom-cat!
Grimes He'll be a damn sight muckier an' all before the day is out.
Housemaid I wouldn't 'ave thought he could have got any muckier—there's nowhere else on 'im for muck to stick. Just look at him . . .

Song 3A: Never Seen Anything (Reprise)

(*Singing*) Well, I'll take you behind
Out of sight out of mind
And I hope I don't find
You're the thieving kind
Oh, I've never seen anything
Quite so nasty
In the days and months and years of my natural life!

The music continues behind as the Housemaid escorts Tom and Grimes towards the house and we go to:

Scene 4

Harthover Hall

We are in the drawing-room at Harthover Hall—although we will not need to see much more of it than the ornate fireplace and, possibly, a couple of pieces of furniture covered with dustsheets

The Housemaid ushers in Grimes and Tom who is carrying sacking and brushes and gazes around, open-mouthed

Housemaid You will watch where you're putting your feet, won't you? And you'll keep your hands off the furniture and walls?
Grimes (*cuffing Tom*) Are you listening? D'y'hear what she's telling you, you gormless young monkey?
Tom Ow! That hurt!
Grimes It was meant to hurt. Don't you worry, miss, I'll see that the little beggar behaves his-self. I'll keep my eye on him.

Grimes has taken a bottle out of his pocket and now takes a swig at the contents. He belches and then realizes that the Housemaid is watching him

Medicinal, miss—that's what that is—purely medicinal. I 'as to take it, like it or not—even though I 'ates the taste of the stuff. It's the soot what

does it, you see. It gets inside the bronchial tubes and lungs.
Housemaid Well I never.
Grimes I'm a martyr to my bronchial tubes and lungs, miss, and all because of a lifetime lived in soot. (*He snatches the sacking and some metal weights from out of Tom's hands*) Give us ho'd of that tackle, lad—and don't stand gawping. And shut your gob. You're here to sweep chimbleys, not stand around catching flies. You can get off about your business, miss, and leave the rest to me.
Housemaid I can't. I wish I could. I've got my orders. I'm to stop in here, until you're done, and see that nothing comes to any harm.
Grimes Harm? Why, what could come to harm in here? The entire contents of this room are in the capable hands of a master-sweep—— (*At which point, he knocks an ornament off the mantelpiece with his elbow*) Get that!

Tom makes a hopeless attempt at catching the ornament as it crashes to the floor. Grimes aims a blow at him yet again

You cack-handed clumsy good-for-nothing! Get yourself up that chimbley where you can do less damage!

Grimes begins to attach the sacking in front of the fireplace with the weights as Tom takes off his jacket preparatory to climbing the chimney

Housemaid Is he really going to go up there? (*To Tom*) Are yer?

Tom nods. She peers up the fireplace

It's ever so dark—aren't you scared?
Grimes He's more scared of what he'll get if he doesn't go—the toe-end of my boot up his backside. Up with you, lad.

Tom, carrying a brush, sets off up the chimney

The Housemaid peers up as he goes

Housemaid It's ever so narrow!
Grimes You'll need to get your head away from there, miss—unless it's a face full of soot you're after.

As the Housemaid moves away Grimes continues to cover the fireplace with the sacking

Housemaid Does he ever get stuck?
Grimes Not him! Not Tom! He slips up chimbleys as easy as a rat along a drain pipe. (*He calls up the fireplace*) How goes it, lad?
Tom (*off, calling back*) Not bad, master! Except it twists and turns a lot!
Grimes It will do, lad—they twists and turns all over the place, the chimbleys in these old houses! (*He turns back to the Housemaid*) He's a natural-born chimbley sweep's apprentice is that lad. He's thin, d'y'see. He's all skin-and-bone—he's weedy. I hand-picked that boy myself from the parish. To a master chimbley-sweep, such as myself, that lad is worth his weight in soot.
Housemaid What if he starts to get fat?

Grimes He won't.
Housemaid 'Oo says?
Grimes I does.
Housemaid Get on with you!
Grimes It's true. (*Calling up the fireplace again*) How goes it now?
Tom (*off, from further away*) Still going—except I cannot see my hand in front of my face!
Grimes (*back to the Housemaid*) Would I lie to you? Prize-fighters and strong-men you builds up—chimbley-sweeps apprentices you thins down. It's an art, it is, is keeping a chimbley-sweep's apprentice trim—a reg'lar art.
Housemaid I'll bet it is.
Grimes There's some comestibles they mustn't get too much of, for a start. And meat they must not have at any cost.
Housemaid Fancy that!
Grimes I can safely place my hand on my heart and give you my solemn assurance, here and now, that red meat has never touched that little lad's lips.
Housemaid Well I never!
Grimes Nor fancy-cakes nor pastries neither.
Housemaid What does he get then?
Grimes The leavings off my plate for a start. Bits of bread and cabbage-stalks—boiled pertaters soaked in gravy, sort of thing.
Housemaid It's plain to see you have his interest at heart.
Grimes I have to, miss. And it's not just a question of keeping him thinned down, d'y'see? It's keeping him thinned down and yet keeping his mind supple.
Housemaid Go on! It don't require much brain-work, going up and down a chimbley.
Grimes You think again. You needs to be quick-witted when you're up there in the dark. They're reg'lar rabbit-warrens, some of these chimbley-stacks. Twisting and turning then doubling back upon themselves. A lad that hasn't got his wits about him, can quite easily come down a different chimbley to the one that he went up. And then there's trouble. (*He calls up the chimney again*) How goes it now?

There is no reply

Tom! *Tom!* Do you hear me, lad! Answer me, if you know what's good for you! (*Then, solemnly, to the Housemaid*) What did I say? He's gone!
Housemaid Gone?
Grimes Gone down the wrong chimbley! The careless clumsy little wretch! (*He removes the sacking from the fireplace and puts his head up the chimney*) Tom! *Tom!* Are you up there? Do you—— (*He breaks off as he dissolves into a fit of coughing—when his head comes back into view, we see that his face is covered in soot*)

The Housemaid is overtaken by a fit of giggles

It's all his fault—I'll knock his head clean off his shoulders when I do lay hold of him . . .

Then, we go into a total Black-out as we hear Tom calling out in the pitch-black of the chimney

Tom's voice Master! Master! It's terrible black up here, master—I think I've taken a wrong turning! Mr Grimes! Are you there, Mr Grimes? . . . Ho'd on! I can see a bit of light! I think I've found it, master—I'm coming down again . . .

And the Lights come up slowly on:

Scene 5

Ellie's Bedroom

A small neat bedroom which is "all dressed in white; white bed-curtains, white furniture, white walls, with just a few lines of pink here and there" NB: I am assuming that the fireplace in the drawing-room will revolve to provide the bedroom fireplace. Apart from this main structure the rest of the room need only be hinted at, although of course, we shall need a window for Tom's exit. There is also a bed; a cheval mirror; and a wash-stand on which there sits a wash-bowl; a water-jug; a face-flannel; soap; nail-brush, etc.

A girl, Ellie, is fast asleep on the bed, which, ideally, should be a four-poster. Ellie is about Tom's age (although she could be a couple of years older), she has cheeks "that are almost as white as the pillow and her hair is like threads of gold and spread about all over the bed"

Tom enters, scrambling down the chimney and is, at first, taken aback—he stands gazing around, open-mouthed, in wonder and surprise. He has not yet noticed Ellie asleep on the bed

Tom Hey up, Tom lad, you don't belong in here—and the sooner you go back the way you came, the better—else Grimes'll skin thee alive . . . (*He moves to go back up the chimney-piece but stops as his attention is held by a framed picture above the mantelpiece and then he looks around the room again*) It won't harm though, to stop for a minute . . . (*He wanders around the room, reaching out at objects but not daring to touch them for fear of soiling them. He half speaks, half-sings to a slow tempo*)

Song 3B: Never Seen Anything (Reprise)

I've never seen anything quite so white
Anywhere I've been
It's a palace I'm in . . .
And it's fit for a queen
It's so clean . . .
Must be having a dream!

I wonder who it does belong to? (*He arrives at the wash-stand*) And look at all this here—soap and towels and jugs of watter. If it's right what Mr Grimes says, only mucky folk wash, it must be a right proper mucky devil that lives in here! And where does all the dirt go after who-ever-it-is has washed theirselves? There's not so much as a speck of muck on these towels ... (*He turns from the wash-stand and then pulls up, startled into immobility for the moment, at his first glimpse of Ellie asleep on the bed, then*)

By heck it's a lass ... !
With ribbons and curls ...
(*Speaking*) Or is it a doll ... ?
Nay—a real live girl ...
Eh, I've never seen anything quite as lovely
In all my life ...

But surely all that soap and watter and towels and stuff are not for her? Why, she's that clean, I'll swear she's never needed a wash since the day she was born! Or happen she just had a wash afore she went to sleep ... Ay, that'll be it—are all folk as clean as that just after they've had a wash? Eh, I wish I was as clean as she is ... ! (*He stares glumly at his own grimy hands and arms and attempts to rub some of the dirt off but, having no success, gives up*) You've no right to be in here, Tom, lad, not with her lying there in that bed—they'll do more than skin thee alive if tha's caught in here! (*And he turns again to leave but this time comes face to face with his own image in the cheval mirror. He stands for a moment, as though frozen again, not recognizing this stranger—then he puts out a hand and touches the mirror*) It's me—I thought it were another lad—God, am I really as mucky as that ... ? (*With which, he stumbles towards the fireplace in order to make his exit but, in his haste, he knocks over the fire-irons which clatter noisily in the hearth*)

Ellie wakes and sits up, startled, on the bed. For a moment, the boy and the girl hold each other's gaze—equally terrified. Tom is the first to recover his senses

It's all right, miss—I shall not hurt you——

But the sound of Tom's voice only serves to jerk Ellie into life and she begins to scream at the top of her voice

Ellie Help! Help!
Tom Don't shout, miss—I'm only the sweep's lad—I wouldn't do you any harm——
Ellie Help, nurse! Help!

Ellie continues to scream and, at the sound of approaching footsteps, Tom spots the open window and rushes towards it

The door bursts open and Ellie's Nurse, a stout middle-aged woman, enters

Nurse Whatever's the matter, Miss Ellie——

She breaks off as she catches sight of Tom who is half-in and half-out of the window and then she too begins to scream

Tom makes his exit

As the Lights dim and the set is struck, several figures enter downstage, separately and possibly carrying lanterns, and peer around—these include: Sir John; the Housemaid; the Gamekeeper; the Nurse—and any other members of the cast who may be available and dressed as more of Sir John's employees (possibly a Gardener and a Dairymaid)

Sir John What's amiss? What's all the screaming about?
Housemaid There's a man climbed into Miss Ellie's bedroom!
Nurse A demon more like—I saw him with my own eyes!
Gamekeeper I caught sight of him in the grounds—running as fast as his legs might carry him!
Gardener Making off with the contents of the master's safe, as like as not!
Housemaid Absconding with the mistress's jewel-case, I shouldn't wonder!
Nurse Tread carefully—he's six foot tall if he's an inch!
Housemaid And armed to the teeth as well!
Gamekeeper I dunno about him being six foot tall—he looked more like a ragamuffin to me.
Sir John An intruder all the same—he must be caught!

At which point, Tom hares across the stage, evading their clutches, and disappearing again, as:

Housemaid There he goes!
Gardener After him!
Sir John Bring that boy to me!

The set clears as we go into a choreographed "chase" number in which Sir John and his servants pursue Tom in all directions

During the chase, the Irishwoman appears on separate occasions and at separate places, and indicates to Tom which direction to take. Then, as the pursuers return, she points off in a different direction, sending them the wrong way. We will also discover that the Irishwoman is nimbler, and younger, than she had appeared in her previous scene

Song 4: Stop That Lad

Household Stop that lad—he's been bad!
Stop that wretch—fetch, dogs, fetch!
Stop that lad—the lad's been bad!
Call out the hounds. Halloo!
Catch that child. The child is wild
Come join the hullaballoo
Chasing over the garden
Chasing over the lawn
Racing over the meadow

Through the acres of corn
Stop that lad—the boy's been bad
He's robbed us—terrible thief
Comb the ground until he's found
He's brought us nothing but grief
Someone call for the justice
Quick he mustn't be late
Where's the law when we need it

Sir John But I'm the magistrate!

Irishwoman That way, boy!

Harmony Pace. Race. Chase. Stop the lad!
Pace. Race. Chase. Stop the lad!
Racing. Chasing. Makes us hopping mad!
Racing. Chasing. Makes us hopping mad!
Face fair cop! You've been bad.
Face fair cop! You've been bad.

Irishwoman This way and you'll lose them.

Household Stop the brat and put the rat
In gaol where he belongs
We don't like a dirty tyke
Who can't tell right from wrong
Racing over the moorland
Chase is driving us mad
Feet are blistered and sore and
No more breath to be had
But we'll still catch him, by gad!
Stop that lad!
Stop that lad!

And they fade into silence as they exit on wing

Stop that lad!

The chase might have taken us into the audience and then back on to the darkening stage for a final chorus then, as the Pursuers exit, the Irishwoman appears again and, hovering in the shadows, calls out, softly

Irishwoman This way! It's safe now! This way, Tom—there is nothing for you to fear.

Tom enters, bedraggled and exhausted. He cannot see the Irishwoman who is invisible to him

Tom Who calls me? Who calls my name? Where are you? *Who* are you? And why have you led me here? And where is it that you have brought me?

Irishwoman You'll find out, Tom. All in good time. Goodbye.

Tom Don't go! Don't leave me!

Irishwoman I must. There is other work that I must do.

Tom What kind of work?

Irishwoman Smoothing sick folks' pillows, whispering sweet dreams in their ears; opening cottage casements, to let in God's good air; coaxing little children away from gutters and foul pools where fever breeds—doing all I can to help those who will not help themselves. Remember Tom—those that wish to be clean, clean they will be—and those that wish to be foul, foul they will be.

With which, the Irishwoman moves back into the darkness

Tom is left alone. With him, we hear the sound of church bells far away in the distance

Tom Church bells? Then is it Sunday? But if it *is* Sunday, and yesterday was Thursday, what happened to Friday? Whatever became of Saturday?

Tom shakes his head then rubs his ears with his hands, and listens again. But the bells have gone

And now they're gone again. I wish I knew what day it was. I wish I knew where I was. I wish I didn't feel so alone. (*He looks down at his grimy hands and arms again and, again, tries to rub away the dirt*) I wish I was *clean*!

The moment is pointed up, musically, then:

Irishwoman's voice Those that wish to be clean, Tom, clean they shall be!

And the Lights come up on:

Scene 6

The Cottage By The River

We are outside a picture-book cottage with roses and clematis around the door. There is a small outhouse at one side of the cottage and, perhaps, a white-painted garden fence in front

Outside the front-door of the cottage, sitting in a rocking-chair and reading a book or performing some domestic task is "the nicest Old Woman that ever was seen, in a red petticoat, short dimity bedgown, and clean white cap with a black silk handkerchief over it, tied under her chin". There is a stool at the side of her chair on which there stands a jug of milk, a cup, and a plate containing fresh bread

Tom crosses wearily towards the cottage

Tom Missis! Please, missis!

Old Woman (*rising*) What art thou? And what dost thou want? Why—you're a sweep's lad, aren't you? Away with thee! I'll have no sweeps here!

Tom Give us a cup of watter, missis.

Old Woman Water, is it? There's water a-plenty in the river round the back. Be off with you!

Tom But I cannot go a step farther, missis. Not without a drink. Please, missis. I'm that tired and hungry and my throat's fair parched.

Tom sways unsteadily and the Old Woman rushes to support him

Old Woman God forgive me! He's sick—and a bairn's a bairn, chimney-sweep or not. (*She helps him to the rocking-chair*) Sit thee down, child.

Tom And can I have a sip of watter then?

Old Woman Water's bad for thee. (*She pours out milk into the cup*) Here—take that, it's today's milk. And look—here's bread to go with it as well.

Tom drinks

Where didst thou come from?

Tom (*pointing upwards*) From over there. Then down yon Fell.

Old Woman Across from Harthover? Thou didn't!

Tom I did an' all!

Old Woman What and in the dark and by thy self?

Tom nods

Art sure thou art not lying?

Tom Why should I?

Old Woman And how got ye up there in the first place?

Tom I went there with my master. I was at Harthover Hall. We went to clean the chimneys.

Old Woman Bless thy little heart! And you ran away? You haven't been stealing, have you, from Sir John?

Tom I wouldn't.

Old Woman Bless thy little heart. I'll warrant not. Why dost thou not eat thy bread?

Tom I can't.

Old Woman It's good enough, for I made it myself.

Tom I can't. Tell me something?

Old Woman If I can?

Tom Is it Sunday?

Old Woman No of course it's not—why should it be?

Tom As I was coming here, I thought I heard the church-bells ringing—and then again, a moment since, I thought I heard them again.

Old Woman Bless thy pretty heart! There are no bells ringing here, child—unless they be ringing in your head, or else it's the river tinkling past. You need to rest. I'll find you somewhere out of the sun. If thou wert a shade cleaner, I'd take thee into the house and put thee in my own bed, for the Lord's sake. Can you bear to stand?

Tom nods and rises, unsteadily

Then come thee here with me.

Tom Is there somewhere I can wash myself?

Old Woman Mercy, lad there'll be time for washing after you wake, it's sleep you need the most.
Tom Those that wish to be clean, the lady said, clean they shall be.
Old Woman As soon as you awake, I'll fetch you water in a bowl myself. (*She has led him over to the outhouse and now opens the door*) In here—it's not much, I'll grant you, but it's dry, at least, and there is soft sweet hay to lie on.
Tom And afterwards you promise I'll be clean?
Old Woman None cleaner, child—I promise. But first you must rest.

And Tom allows himself to be ushered into the out-house

The Old Woman closes the door of the outhouse, then crosses, picks up the milk-jug, cup and plate and goes inside the cottage

A moment later, Sir John enters accompanied by the Gamekeeper

The following eight lines are spoken under improvised accompaniment

Sir John Must find that boy and bring him back
Back where the lad belongs
Gamekeeper Anyone can make mistakes
I fear we've done the lad wrong
Sir John Tell me, whose is this cottage?
Gamekeeper The old school-mistress, Sir John
Sir John Knock then, man, and we'll ask here
Must find the lad before long.

The Gamekeeper knocks on the cottage door in the rhythm of the last line

The Old Woman comes out. She gives Sir John a low curtsy

(*Speaking*) Well, dame, and how are you?
Old Woman Blessings on you as broad as your back, Harthover, and welcome into Vendale: but you're not hunting the fox at this time of the year?
Sir John No—but I am hunting, and strange game too. I'm looking for a lost child, a chimney-sweep that is run away.
Old Woman Oh, Harthover, Harthover, you were always a just and merciful man, and you'll promise me you'll not harm the poor little lad if I give you tidings of him?
Sir John *Harm* him? That's the last thing that's in my mind.
Gamekeeper Sir John wants only to find the boy in order to help him, not hurt him.
Sir John We mistook him for a housebreaker or thief—when all that had really happened was that the poor lad lost his way inside a chimney and came down into the wrong room.
Old Woman So he told me the truth then, the poor little dear!
Sir John He told you? Then you have seen him? You know where he is?
Old Woman He's safe. He's here.
Sir John Thanks be to God! We've been all across the moors since early morning. I've men now along the river-bank. Whereabouts is the boy?

The Old Woman has crossed to the outhouse and now opens the door and peers inside

Old Woman Gone!
Sir John Gone where?
Old Woman I know not where—ten minutes since I watched him myself as he laid his little head down on this straw—and now he's gone.
Gamekeeper Which way?
Old Woman There's a broken window at the back, he must have clambered through.
Gardener (*off*) Sir John! Mr Burrell, are you about?
Gamekeeper Here, Raistrick! In the lane!

The Gardener enters from behind the cottage, carrying a neat pile of clothing: Tom's trousers, socks, shirt, boots, etc.

Gardener I came across these, Sir John.
Sir John Where?
Gardener Just round the back, laid out on the river-bank as neat as if somebody had gone in for a swim—except there ain't sight nor sign of who they might belong to.

Sir John, having taken the clothing from the Gardener, shows it to the Old Woman

Sir John Is it the boy's?

The Old Woman thumbs through the articles and shakes her head signifying that she cannot be sure

Gamekeeper Look inside the britches-pockets—happen you'll find something there that'll tell you, Sir John.

Sir John feels inside the pockets, pulls out what is in them

Sir John Three marbles; a brass button with string tied to it—nothing more.
Old Woman God forgive me, but the child was that anxious only to be clean, and I never gave a thought to it. "Mayn't I be clean?" he said—those were his words. And all that I had the sense to tell him was: "Later, later".
Sir John Did you look down into the river-bottom?
Gardener It's too deep to *see* the bottom, Sir John—and fast flowing with it. If he tried to bathe in there, he'd be carried downstream and drowned for sure.
Sir John The poor lad's gone then.

There is a pause. The morning sunlight darkens into shadow and there is the sonorous tolling of church bells close at hand. The Old Woman, Sir John, the Gamekeeper and the Gardener stand motionless for several seconds, then:

If we cannot give the child an honest proper Christian burial, at least we can bow our heads and say a prayer for him.

They have been joined by the Housemaid and the Nurse, both wearing black shawls over their heads

As the church-bells continue to toll, the Lights fade to a Black-out as the gauze is lowered and we go to:

Scene 7

A Country Churchyard

Which is represented by a gravestone which is, perhaps, standing in the shade of a willow-tree

We open on Ellie as she lays some flowers on the grave, sobbing quietly to herself

The Irishwoman enters

Irishwoman Child . . . child! Why are you crying?
Ellie For the chimney-sweep's boy.
Irishwoman He doesn't lie beneath that gravestone.
Ellie He hasn't got a gravestone. He hasn't even got a grave. No-one knows where the poor lad lies—they never found his body. And so each day I come down into the churchyard and choose a different grave—and pretend that it's his.
Irishwoman And why, pray, would you do that?
Ellie So that I can mourn him.
Irishwoman Mourn him indeed! And what's a common chimney-sweep's lad to a fine well-brought up young lady like yourself? Why should you choose to mourn him?
Ellie Because it was my fault that he drowned.
Irishwoman And who told you that?
Ellie If I had not screamed at the sight of him, there would not have been a chase, if there had been no chase he would not have gone down Lewthwaite Crag, and if he had not gone down Lewthwaite Crag he would never have gone near the river—and if he had not gone to the river, he would still be alive today.
Irishwoman And who says he's not alive still?
Ellie Why—everybody does.
Irishwoman Am I not one of that everybody? And I don't tell you that he's drowned.
Ellie Who are you that says he's still alive?
Irishwoman A good friend of his—and yours too if you would believe it.
Ellie And is he alive then? Oh, please, please, let him be alive!
Irishwoman Dry your eyes child. He is alive and well.
Ellie May I see him? Can you take me to him?
Irishwoman One day, perhaps—not yet awhile.
Ellie Why can't I see him? Where is he?

Irishwoman In the river still.
Ellie Then he *is* drowned—and you're playing a cruel trick on me.
Irishwoman I have told you that he's alive, and if I say he is, then you must believe it's so.
Ellie But *where* is he?
Irishwoman He has gone to join the Water Babies.
Ellie Water Babies? I've never heard of such a thing.
Irishwoman My dear child, there are a great many things in the world which you have never heard of—and a great many things which nobody ever heard of—and a great many things too, which nobody will ever hear of—but you must take my word for it that they exist.
Ellie Is the chimney-sweep's boy happy with these Water Babies?
Irishwoman He is happier than he was before, but then he does not remember what it was like before—or how *un*happy he was then. He has forgotten most of the past.
Ellie Has he forgotten me?
Irishwoman That remains to be seen. But he does not remember having ever been dirty—or tired, or hungry, or having been beaten by a cruel master, or sent up dark chimneys. But he is not entirely happy, for there are things he has to do, down there, before he can find true happiness.
Ellie I don't believe that I shall ever be happy again. And I don't believe one word that you have told me. (*She begins to sob again*)
Irishwoman In that case, child, it is better that you sleep. Sleep easy, Ellie, with no bad dreams of drownded chimney-sweep little lads to disturb your slumbers. Sleep . . . Sleep . . . (*She makes a few mysterious passes with one hand*)
Ellie I do feel a little drowsy.
Irishwoman Then go to sleep and dream of a world beneath the waters where fishes swim and otters dive and fairies play and little children are turned into Water Babies . . .

Over which, the Lights dim, losing Ellie who falls asleep as the Irishwoman beckons the audience with her as she moves into UV lighting, and:

Scene 8

The River-Bed

Where we are under the water and on the bed of the river with waving water-reeds and perhaps a few boulders, as the Irishwoman sings

Song 5: Come With Me

Irishwoman Come with me to a world that's new
For the children who lived a life of despair and pain
And if you can believe it's true
You'll see Water Babies
My little ones born again

As the song continues, a number of puppet fishes swim into view, weaving in and out of the water-reeds

Gliding down river
Riding the waves
That race to the open sea
Here is a world of mystery
For children to discover
Like other worlds there's danger too
With monsters to find if you dare
From here to the end of nowhere
Our world is like no other
Come down, Tom
And leave the world up there behind
Come and join the Water Babies
Seek and you shall find

Here he comes now—and find the Water Babies he will, but not quite yet awhile—and neither is it time for him to see me either . . . Those that wish to be foul, foul they will be—those that wish to be clean, clean they *shall* be!

At which point, Tom enters, as the UV lighting is replaced by a general state and the Irishwoman moves off. He is now spotlessly clean as is his clothing. He is examining himself in some excitement as he makes a glorious discovery

Tom Hey! What's happened to me? I'm clean!

Song 6: I'm Clean!

(*Singing*) I'm clean! Look see!
I don't understand how it came to be
I thought that I would always be dirty
Now I seem to be clean
Just look. My skin
Is quite as bright as a brand new pin
Even the mucky shirt I was wearing gleams.
(*Speaking*) Look at me! I'm clean!
Just feel as though I've been hurled
Into a bright blue world that's new
To start life again. Just yesterday when
It was raining soot and paining me
Climbing dark and narrow chim-be-leys, then,
I didn't dare dream I'd be C-L-E-A-N!

A pair of Water-Otters enter

Depending upon availability, as the song continues, Tom and the otters may be joined by more River Creatures to augment the Act One Finale

Otters	What's that human? Say it again!
Tom	C-L-E-A-N! I'm clean!
Otters	Of course you are.
	What else would you be if you're underwater?
	Stupid young beggar!
Tom	I never thought a beggar ought to be clean.
Otters	That's quite absurd!
	Ridiculous boy! And where have you heard
	That fish and birds and otters with fur
	Are dirty? Never! We're clean!
	Never judge another being who
	Lives a diff'rent life from you.
	If you do you'll never have seen
	All the wonders that there are to see
	Grow to be just what you want to be, free
Tom	And what's more to me is
	I'm C-L-E-A-N. I'm clean!
	And I know that clean has a special meaning.
Otters	Clean! It's a lovely feeling.
Tom	Clean! And my head is reeling.
All	We could jump clean through the ceiling
Male Otter	If there was one!
All	Clean! For a new beginning.
	New hopes on which we're pinning everything
Tom	And I'm winning!
All	Bells are ringing like a wedding
	New adventures lie ahead
	If people up there say "He's dead"
	They're wrong. They don't need to weep.
	I've/he's made a clean, clean sweep.
Tom	I'm clean!

CURTAIN

ACT II

Scene 1

The River-Bed

Where we are again under the water and back with Tom who, within the number, sets off to explore his surroundings as the Irishwoman enters from the opposite side. As she sings, we go to UV lighting and a number of Water Baby puppets "swim" into view

Song 7: Welcome, Tom (Reprise of Song 5)

Irishwoman Welcome, Tom, to the river wide
On the evening tide
Where the fish dart through moonbeams bright
Where salmon run in the morning sun
And the otters dive
In the mists of the evening light
Go and explore a new kind of life
Where the water is crystal and clean
Down from the mountain stream it flows
To find the winding river

Tom has by now disappeared

And there on the banks the fairies play
With laughter like tinkling glass
They pass on their way with messages
From glow-worms to deliver
Here the mysteries of magic are unfurl'd
Welcome to the secrets of the Water Babies' world ...

(*Speaking*) Well then, my Water Babies, and have you missed me?

Water Babies Where have you been, ma'am, where have you been?

Irishwoman All across the land-world, my little ones, comforting the ailing and reassuring the unhappy—and, lately, I've been attending to a grieving girl who wept because she thought a chimney-sweep's lad was drowned.

Water Babies Where is he now, mother, where is he now?

Irishwoman Why—down here, of course, where else? And how could he have drowned when I have watched safely over him all the time? His name is Tom—and he is to be your brother.

We hear tinkling joyful laughter from the Water Babies at this news

But he is not to meet you yet, mind, or even to know that you are here.

There is still a lot that he has to learn and much that he has to do. Off with you, children, before he gets here. And remember—you must not speak to him, nor let him so much as catch a glimpse of you—only see to it that he is never harmed. Away you go!

As the Water Babies swim off, the Lights change from UV to general

Tom enters from the opposite direction. He pulls up with surprise at seeing the Irishwoman

Irishwoman Come here then and stand close to me—don't be afraid.
Tom Who are you? Haven't I seen you somewhere before?
Irishwoman Perhaps you have and, then again, perhaps you haven't—the fact that I'm here now, Tom, is all that matters.
Tom Tom? Is that what I'm called?
Irishwoman Tom is your name.
Tom (*trying it out*) Tom? Tom! But *what* am I? Was it you that brought me here? And why have I got arms and legs, like you, when all around me have got fins and tails? Where did I come from? What is this place?
Irishwoman Where you came from is in the past—and where you are at this moment is of little consequence. It's where you are going, Tom, that's important.
Tom But I don't know where I'm going—can you tell me?
Irishwoman You're setting out on a journey, Tom.
Tom Where to? Is it far away?
Irishwoman As far away as it's possible to go—you must find the Other-End-Of-Nowhere.
Tom The Other-End-Of-Nowhere? Why?
Irishwoman All that will become clear, Tom, once you arrive. (*She waves to Tom as she moves off, into the darkness*) Don't be afraid—you may not always be able to see me—but believe that I'll always be at your side.

She exits

Tom (*waving back*) Goodbye! And don't worry—I'll get there—some way—somehow . . .

But he looks around nervously as the river darkens

The two Water-Otters poke their heads through the weeds at him, intimidatingly

Female Water-Otter You'll get there, I'm sure, provided that you don't get eaten on the way.
Tom Who are you?
Male Water-Otter Don't you know an otter when you see one?
Female Water-Otter Never mind what we are—it's what you are that's most important.
Tom I'm Tom.
Female Water-Otter You're food. A tasty tit-bit, that's what you are!

Tom takes cover behind a boulder

Come out here at once! Come out here and be eaten.

Tom I shan't.

Female Water-Otter You'll do exactly as you're told, or it will be all the worse for you. Come along and be eaten, don't be disobedient.

Tom I'm not coming out! You're not feeding me to anybody!

The Female Water-Otter bares her teeth, snarls, and makes a sudden movement towards Tom

Male Water-Otter Leave it be wife, leave it be. It's not worth eating. It's a newt.

Female Water-Otter (*shivering distastefully*) Oh my goodness me! It isn't, is it?

Male Water-Otter It is I tell you. It's an awful horrible undigestible newt. Nothing eats newts. Not even the vulgar pike at the bottom of the river.

Female Water-Otter A newt! Ugh! There's only one thing nastier than a newt—and that's a sea-urchin. (*To Tom*) They're covered all over with dreadful spiky prickles.

Tom feeling that the immediate danger is over, comes out from his hiding place, feeling at his body

Tom I haven't got any spiky prickles.

Female Water-Otter I didn't say that you had got spiky prickles, newt. Do pay attention. I said you were a newt, newt.

Tom And I'm not a newt either.

Male Water-Otter If we say you're a newt, you are a newt. There's no two ways about it, you're entirely inedible.

Female Water-Otter Perhaps the fishes might eat him—a salmon might fancy a nibble at him.

Tom What's a salmon?

Male Water-Otter Salmon, you ignorant newt, are the lords of the fish and we are the lords of the salmon.

Female Water-Otter They eat the likes of you, grow fat, and then we eat them.

Male Water-Otter That's the way the river runs.

Female Water-Otter Delicious! The children are *very* fond of salmon.

Tom And where are the salmon now? Where do they come from?

Male Water-Otter Out of the sea, of course. The great, wide sea, where they might stay and be safe. But out of the sea the silly things come, and then up the river. And when the rain comes we follow them down again.

Female Water-Otter And it's coming soon! I can smell it now, coming in from the sea. The children *will* be pleased—hurrah for the rain and the fresh salmon and plenty of eating all day long.

Male Water-Otter And tossing and rolling in the breakers and sleeping snug in the warm dry crags along the water's edge.

Female Water-Otter The sea's the most wonderful place in the world to be!

Tom Is the Other-End-Of-Nowhere close to the sea?

Male Water-Otter Everywhere is close to the sea.

Tom Then how can I go there, please? For I have to get to the Other-End-Of-Nowhere.
Female Water-Otter Haven't you heard a word we've said, you stupid eft? Oh, if only you were edible! Wait for the rain and then follow us.
Male Water-Otter Listen!

They all three cock their heads. It is beginning to grow dark overhead

Tom I can't hear anything.
Male Water-Otter Of course you can't! There's nothing to hear.
Tom Then why are we listening?
Male Water-Otter Sssshhh!
Female Water-Otter Not the chirp of a bird.
Male Water-Otter Not the fall of a leaf.
Female Water-Otter Not the snap of a twig.
Male Water-Otter Not a whisper of wind.
Female Water-Otter Everything's still!
Tom Why has it grown so dark?
Male Water-Otter Sssshhh! *Listen*!

And, with them, we hear the "plip-plop" of the first raindrops on the surface of the water

Song 8: Plip Plop

Plip
Female Water-Otter Plop
Male Water-Otter Plip
Female Water-Otter Plop
Male Water-Otter Here comes the rain!
Tom Plip, plop, plip, plop!
Listen again!
Water-Otters Plip, plop, plip, plop!
Louder it comes!
All Plip, plop, plip, plop,
Faster the river runs!

The following will have to be pre-recorded. Over the above the general lighting has decreased to a half black-out, leaving UV as the predominant source, as:

Company Plip, plop, plip, plop, that's all we hear,
Plip, plop, plip, plop, storm's very near,
Plip, plop, plip, plop, suddenly fear,
Plip, plop, time for froggies to disappear!

Plip, plop, plip, plop, bank overflows,
Plip, plop, plip, plop, everyone knows,
Plip, plop, plip, plop, danger and so,
Plip, plop, plip, plop, only one place to go.
Down to the sea,
Faster the river runs,

Down to the sea,
Safety for everyone.
Full of fear we can't stay here
We know instinctively
We must all swim down to the sea

Thunder

Down to the sea—current is very fast
Down to the sea—when will the storm be past?

Lightning

Frogs and fishes,
Otters wish that all of us could be
Quickly, safely, down to the sea

Thunder

Look out for the lightning flash

Lightning

Beware the lightning tree
Quickly, safely, down to the sea

Over the above, we have seen Tom, the Water-Otters and as many other puppet-fish as possible, making their way towards the sea

Suddenly, the puppet fish and the Water-Otters are gone as a warm overhead light of the sun overtakes the darkness and UVs, as:

Tom Down at the sea
Suddenly it's all right
The storm has gone
Darkness has turned to light
Sun is shining
Now I know the place I had to be
Onward, forwards, down to the sea!

And we go to:

Scene 2

The Edge of the Sea

We are still underwater but with a richer shade of blue and, perhaps, a suggestion of sand on the sea-bed

All is now calm as Tom wanders in and meets the Lobster

Tom Excuse me, is this the Other-End-Of-Nowhere?
Lobster Does it *look* like the Other-End-Of-Nowhere?
Tom I don't know what the Other-End-Of-Nowhere looks like.

Lobster Nothing like this, I hasten to assure you.
Tom Is this the sea then?
Lobster Of course it's the sea. Would I be here if it wasn't?
Tom Are you a salmon?
Lobster Do I *look* like a salmon?
Tom I don't know what a salmon looks like either.
Lobster Nothing like me, I hasten to assure you. Salmon indeed! Haven't you ever seen a lobster before?

Tom shakes his head

Then allow me to enlighten you. You are in the happy—I might say fortunate—I might even go further and say *unique* position of looking at one now. I am a lobster. Lobsters are the most intelligent creatures under the sea and I am the most intelligent lobster of them all. There is no question that I cannot answer. There is no problem that I cannot solve:

Song 9: There's Always an Answer

(*Singing*) Working it out. Finding a way
What other folk work out to-morrow
I already know today. Because . . .

There's always an answer in the end
Whatever the problem there's an answer on that you can depend
Apply a little logic and you'll find my friend
That there's always an answer in the end

You know that silly fishes always swim around in schools?
Whoever needs schools? With so many rules?
Ask a fish to say the alphabet and you would see
That he wouldn't know what's after A, B, C,
When a lobster could tell him immediately
The letters after 'C' is always 'L'

Tom I thought it 'D'
Lobster 'L' for lobster! See?
Listen to a lobster and you'll learn humility. Because . . .
Both There's always an answer in the end
Whatever the problem there's an answer on that you can depend

A short soft-shoe routine continues over instrumental bars to . . .

There's always an answer in the end

Lobster You stupid . . . stupid . . . What did you say you were again?
Tom I . . . er . . . I'm . . . er . . .
Lobster And I'm far too intelligent to waste my time on something that doesn't know what it is. Good day to you!

As the Lobster exits the orchestra plays the final chorus line

Tom Wait! *Wait*! Please don't go! It isn't my fault I can't remember anything. (*Then to himself*) If only I knew *why* I had to get to the Other-End-Of-Nowhere, that might help me to remember where I came from ...?

During the following, the Irishwoman enters, unnoticed by Tom

Perhaps, if I thought *very* hard ... (*He screws up his face and closes his eyes as he tries to concentrate his thoughts*) ... I wasn't always under water, I'm sure of that ... I remember now! I used to be very dirty! And I lived in a world where everything was dark ... That's it! And then, one day, I went into a room where everything was ... oh, so white! ... And there was a girl lying on a bed ...

Irishwoman Ellie, Tom.

Tom Ellie! Who said that? (*He opens his eyes and looks around him but cannot see the Irishwoman who is invisible to him*) Ellie, that was her name! But who was she? And who am I? I wish I knew. And why do I have to get to the Other-End-Of-Nowhere?

Irishwoman Close your eyes, Tom, and think hard again—and much might be revealed to you ...

Tom closes his eyes once more and concentrates. The Lights dim

The Irishwoman exits as we go to:

Scene 3

Harthover Hall

Although all that we see of it, with Tom, is Ellie's four-poster bed which is trucked in. It is night and the only pool of light comes from an oil-lamp which is being held up by the Housemaid. Ellie is lying in bed, ill, and is being attended to by a Doctor. Sir John is hovering anxiously at the bedside

Tom remains apart from the scene, observing it from the shadows on the other side of the stage

The Doctor, who has been sounding Ellie's chest, removes his stethoscope, sighs, shakes his head and shrugs at Sir John hopelessly

Sir John What ails her, doctor?

Doctor If I knew that, Sir John, then I'd know how to begin to cure her. I can find nothing wrong. She's been this way, you say, since the day that a chimney-sweep's apprentice entered this room?

Sir John Ay—that was the day it all began.

Housemaid Poor lamb, she's been in a sad decline from that self-same day to this.

Sir John But could the poor boy's disappearance have affected her this much?

Doctor If she feels herself responsible for whatever happened to him, yes—where is he now?

Housemaid Drowned, doctor—dead and drowned for sure.
Sir John We searched high and low along that river bank without a trace—and were forced to give him up for lost.
Doctor If only he could be brought to life again then!
Sir John Is his well-being *that* important for my daughter's recovery?
Doctor If my assumption is correct, Sir John, and the girl's condition has been brought about by her belief, however misguided, that she was responsible for the chimney-sweep lad's death—then, yes, I'm sure there would be an instant improvement in her condition if that boy could be found and proved to be alive and well.
Sir John And if *my* assumption is correct, doctor, and the unfortunate lad is drowned, then one might search from here as far as the other-end-of-nowhere and yet not bring him back to life.
Doctor Indeed one might, Sir John, indeed one might . . .

Over the Doctor's words, the four-poster is trucked off as the Lights dim again and Tom moves into a spot, as:

Tom I'm here! I'm not dead at all! Don't go! Please stay!

But the bed has gone, together with the group clustered around it. Tom continues to himself

As far as the Other-End-Of-Nowhere, that's what the squire said. Perhaps that's why I've got to go there—perhaps that's how Ellie's to be saved. And, if that's the case, I must set out right away . . .

Song 10: The Other-End-Of-Nowhere

(*Singing*) The Other-End-Of-Nowhere? Tell me, which way does it lie
And if I ever get there, will I know the reason why?
The Other-End-Of-Nowhere sounds a long long way away
Will it take until tomorrow or for ever and a day?

The Irishwoman enters

Irishwoman The Other-End-Of-Nowhere. Yes, Tom, now's the time to start and if you are to find it you must look inside your heart
The Other-End-Of-Nowhere seems a long long way from here
But with love and hope to guide you you may find it very near
Both The Other-End-Of-Nowhere on the great adventure trail
With friends always beside you how could anybody fail
The journey's full of dangers and sometimes it may be slow
But the Other-End-Of-Nowhere
Tom Is I know where I must go
Irishwoman The Other-End-Of-Nowhere
Tom Now I know
Irishwoman The Other-End-Of-Nowhere

Tom Here I go
Irishwoman The Other-End-Of-Nowhere
Tom Yes, I dare to
Both Find the Other-End-Of-Nowhere

Scene 4

Under the Sea

And the lighting comes up on the Lobster who is now trapped inside a lobster-pot on the sea-bed. There is a rock which will later prove to be a cupboard

Tom Hullo again.
Lobster Never mind the introductory formalities. Don't just stand there, whatever-you-call-yourself—help me to get out.
Tom I should think, if you're as clever as you say you are, you ought to be able to get out by yourself.
Lobster I can't get out.
Tom Why did you get in?
Lobster After a piece of nasty horrible dead fish that somebody had put in here.
Tom What piece of fish? Show it to me!
Lobster I can't—I've eaten it.
Tom How did you get in?
Lobster Through that round hole at the end.
Tom Then why don't you get out the same way?
Lobster Because I can't. I have jumped upwards, downwards, and sideways, at least four thousand times each and I can't get out. It's impossible.
Tom It doesn't look impossible to me—from where I'm standing, it looks quite easy.
Lobster It looked extremely easy to me as well—when I was standing where you are. Once you're inside, it's an altogether different problem. Getting in *is* easy, it's getting *out* that presents the difficulty.
Tom Supposing I put my arm inside and take hold of your claw and help you out—like this ... be careful!

Tom has put an arm inside the lobster-pot but the Lobster, in its anxiety, is threshing and rolling about, almost dragging Tom inside as well. Tom's protestations and the Lobster's complainings will be best extemporized during rehearsals—but, when their struggling is at its peak, they are both brought suddenly to a halt by a sharp cry

As Mrs Bedonebyasyoudid enters

Mrs Bedonebyasyoudid Stop that at once, the pair of you!

Tom and the Lobster do as they are told. They look across, in some trepidation, at the woman who has just entered. Mrs Bedonebyasyoudid is a formidable lady who: "wears a black bonnet, a black shawl, and no crinoline at all; and a pair of large green spectacles, and a great hooked nose. She carries a birch-cane under her arm."

Disgraceful! You should both be positively ashamed of yourselves! Creating all those waves and making all that fuss! Don't you know that there are fishes trying to *bask*—to say nothing of the Water Babies that are taking their afternoon snooze. What under water do you think you're doing?

Tom Please missis, the lobster's got himself trapped in this thing.

Mrs Bedonebyasyoudid That "thing", child, is a lobster-pot—and that particular lobster is continually getting himself trapped in them. Will you *never* learn, you foolish creature? Well? And what do you have to say for yourself?

Lobster I'm extremely sorry, ma'am, but I can't get out.

Mrs Bedonebyasyoudid You never can get out, lobster. And why can't you get out this time?

Lobster Please, ma'am, because it's not possible.

Mrs Bedonebyasyoudid Nonsense! I explained it all to you most carefully yesterday—and the day before and the day before the day before yesterday as well! What you are looking for, lobster, is an exit—when all that a lobster-pot contains is an entrance—so, what is it that we do in such a circumstance?

Lobster Don't know, ma'am, begging your pardon.

Mrs Bedonebyasyoudid "Don't know"! "Don't know"? Don't know indeed! "Don't know was made to know, can't learn was taught to!" We turn ourselves round, backwards, and go out as if we were coming in. It's all perfectly simple. Don't just *stand* there, child, help him!

Tom Yes, missis!

Tom assists the Lobster and guides it, backwards, out of the lobster-pot

Mrs Bedonebyasyoudid There! Could anything be simpler than that?

Lobster No, ma'am.

Song 11: There's Always an Answer (Reprise)

Mrs Bedonebyasyoudid You see there's always an answer in the end
Whatever the problem there's an answer
On that you can depend
Apply a little logic and you'll find, my friend
That there's always an answer in the end

(*Speaking*) Understood?

Lobster Yes, ma'am.

Mrs Bedonebyasyoudid I doubt it.

(*Singing*) Do you imagine there's a chance that in your head
you'd store
The memory for a single day more
None whatever!

In one feeler—out the other side!
You don't think because you're so puffed up with pride
But pride will always come before a fall
And now my patience you have really tried!

Lobster I feel so small

Mrs Bedonebyasyoudid
(*Speaking*) You know I'd call
You, of all the sea-creatures, the stupidest of all!

What are you, lobster? Answer me!

Lobster Of all the sea-creatures, ma'am?

Mrs Bedonebyasyoudid Mmmm?

Lobster The stupidest of all.

Mrs Bedonebyasyoudid Correct. Now, off you go and be quick about it before I *thoroughly* lose my temper . . . !

(*Singing*) Apply a little logic and you'll find my friend
That there's always an answer in the end

The Lobster scuttles off—again, as on its previous exit, it may disappear by sinking behind a rock

Mrs Bedonebyasyoudid rounds on Tom

And as for you! Do you know who I am?

Tom No, missis.

Mrs Bedonebyasyoudid *Ma'am*, child! Not "missis", ma'am! I'm Mrs Bedonebyasyoudid—but to you I'm *ma'am*. Do you know who you are yourself?

Tom If it please you, missis——

He corrects himself as Mrs Bedonebyasyoudid brandishes her cane, threateningly

—if it please you, *ma'am*, a lot of it's coming back to me: I'm called Tom and I used to be a chimney-sweep's lad that worked for a master called Mr Grimes.

Mrs Bedonebyasyoudid And do you know where your Mr Grimes is now?

Tom No, ma'am.

Mrs Bedonebyasyoudid Would it pain you to hear that he, too, had suffered an accident the same as yours and fallen into the river?

Tom (*looking round anxiously*) It would pain me more ma'am, to know that he was about to turn up here.

Mrs Bedonebyasyoudid On that particular you need have no fear—your Mr Grimes was poaching the squire's salmon at the time and is being punished for his crime. What do you know about the Other-End-Of-Nowhere?

Tom Only that I'm to make my way there as fast as possible—is Mr Grimes going to the Other-End-Of-Nowhere too?

Mrs Bedonebyasyoudid All that you will learn, and more, once you arrive—but how do you imagine you will get there quickly if you pause to dawdle with lobsters?
Tom I only stopped to help him out of the lobster-pot.
Mrs Bedonebyasyoudid And tease him too, perhaps, for not being as clever as he said he was? (*She produces a jar of sweets from inside her voluminous clothing*) Do you like sweets?

Tom nods

Come here. Open wide.

Tom opens his mouth and Mrs Bedonebyasyoudid pops something into it. Tom pulls a face and spits the object out

Tom It wasn't a sweet at all—it was a pebble!
Mrs Bedonebyasyoudid That's right.
Tom You are a nasty cruel woman.
Mrs Bedonebyasyoudid And you are a nasty cruel boy who puts pebbles into the sea-anemones' mouths, to take them in and make them fancy that they had caught a good dinner! As you did to them so I must do to you.
Tom Who told you that I'd done that to them?
Mrs Bedonebyasyoudid I am Mrs Bedonebyasyoudid, there's no use trying to hide anything from me—I can read your innermost thoughts, Tom.
Tom What am I thinking now, then?
Mrs Bedonebyasyoudid For one thing, you're thinking that I'm very ugly.

Tom hangs his head

There's nothing to be ashamed about—I am the ugliest fairy in all the world, and so I shall be until people behave themselves as they ought to do. And then I shall grow as handsome as my sister, who is the loveliest fairy in the world; and her name is Mrs Doasyouwouldbedoneby. So she just begins where I end, and I begin where she ends—where I punish, she praises; my sister cherishes where I chastize. (*She holds up her jar of pebbles*) As I dole out sea-pebbles, she dispenses sweetmeats. Can you keep a secret ... ?

Tom nods. Mrs Bedonebyasyoudid crosses to a rock which, at the touch of her hand, moves to reveal itself as a door that swings open. This secret store-cupboard contains row after row of jars of sweets and other enticing things to eat

These are all my sister's things.
Tom I never saw so many sweets! Who are they for?
Mrs Bedonebyasyoudid Why, for the Water Babies, of course, who else? But they are not to be touched by any other person. (*She puts her jar of pebbles on the bottom shelf and then closes the door*) And no-one must ever open this door except my sister or myself—do you understand that, Tom?
Tom Oh, yes.
Mrs Bedonebyasyoudid And do you promise me, on your solemnest oath,

that you will forget this very instant that you even so much as *knew* there was a cupboard there?

Tom I promise, ma'am—but will you do something for me?

Mrs Bedonebyasyoudid Perhaps—if I am able.

Tom Then tell me when I might *see* a Water Baby—for I keep hearing of them, but have never so much as set eyes on one.

Mrs Bedonebyasyoudid Why, child, if that is your dearest wish, then it can be arranged immediately—but mind, for they are mischievous creatures and can sing a song, should they have a mind for it, that could send you straightway off to sleep . . .

The Lights dim and the music fades in behind as Mrs Bedonebyasyoudid moves back into the shadows as:

Cover your ears, Tom, for they are coming now . . .

Mrs Bedonebyasyoudid exits as we go into the UV lighting and the Water Babies puppets enter, covered in a "special" or follow spot downstage

Tom is too excited on seeing them to keep his hands over his ears and obeys the commands in the song

Song 12: Go to Sleep

Water Babies Feeling droopy? Feeling drowsy?
Things are never as bad as they seem
If you have time to dream, so go to sleep.
Feeling snoozy, feeling woozy?
Like a blanket let the waves sweep
Across and draw you deep, deep into sleep.
Feel as though you are floating in a clear blue sky
On clouds of white fluffy foam
Feel as though you are boating on a lake of crystal
Calm and all alone
Not a whisper, not a murmur, not a sound not even a peep
Whilst we in safety keep you. Go to sleep.

At the end of the song, Tom has fallen under the spell and is asleep on the sea-bed

The Water Babies swim off, giggling happily at their success

We lose the UV lighting and return to a general state as Tom wakes from his sleep and:

Tom Where are you, Water Babies? Don't go away—stay with me, please . . . If you were ever here at all—or did I dream you? Was any of it real? Or did I dream up Mrs Bedonebyasyoudid as well? (*He glances around*) There's only one way to find out—if it *was* a dream, then there isn't a cupboard behind that rock. (*He crosses to the rock and hesitates*) But I mustn't touch it, that's what she said . . . But if it *was* a dream, it won't be there—and if it *is* real, I can close it up again . . .

As Tom hesitates, Mrs Doasyouwouldbedoneby enters unseen by him, and stands watching

Mrs Doasyouwouldbedoneby has "the sweetest, kindest, tenderest, funniest, merriest face that anyone ever saw"—she is, in short a complete contrast to her sister in both looks and dress. NB: As the same actress will be doubling these parts (in addition to playing the Irishwoman), Mrs Bedonebyasyoudid and Mrs Doasyouwouldbedoneby will wear "half-masks" over the upper part of their faces

Tom, finally summoning up the courage, opens the "rock-cupboard" and is delighted to discover that he has not been dreaming

So it *was* all real then!

He glances all around but does not see Mrs Doasyouwouldbedoneby who is standing in the shadows

And now that it *is* opened, and there are so many good things inside, it surely would be a pity and a waste not to taste just *one* of them. (*And he lifts out one of the jars, opens it, and crams a sweet into his mouth*)

Mrs Doasyouwouldbedoneby (*to herself*) Ah, you poor little dear! I am afraid that you are just like all the rest.

Tom looks around again, but again, fails to see her—perhaps she is invisible to him at this point? Then, with her, we watch Tom as he hastily stuffs sweets into his mouth from the various jars before returning them to the cupboard and closing the door. Mrs Doasyouwouldbedoneby moves towards him, as:

Well then, and are you the Tom that I have been hearing so much about?

Tom (*turning guiltily*) Ay, missis—are you that other one's sister?

Mrs Doasyouwouldbedoneby Indeed and indeed I am, Tom. I am Mrs Doasyouwouldbedoneby that comforts all small children—come here to me.

Tom crosses to her in some trepidation, but she embraces him warmly

There child, there—and is there something now that you would like to tell me?

Tom No, mum.

Mrs Doasyouwouldbedoneby Think, Tom—think hard—something that you might have done that you should not have done?

Tom Nothing at all as I knows of, mum.

Mrs Doasyouwouldbedoneby Concerning the contents of the cupboard behind that rock over there?

Tom Cupboard, mum? What cupboard might that be? I don't know naught about no cupboards nor nothing what might be in 'em, missis.

Mrs Doasyouwouldbedoneby pushes Tom away

Please, mum, don't leave hold of me—nobody never held me in their arms afore.

Mrs Doasyouwouldbedoneby Tom, Tom—I should dearly like to cuddle you, but I fear I cannot any longer—you have grown prickly and spiky all over.

Tom (*feeling at his face and arms and body in horror*) Eh, missis, why have I gone like that then? What's happened to me?

Mrs Doasyouwouldbedoneby I would rather that *you* told *me* the answer to that, Tom—hast thou been telling lies to anyone?

Tom No, mum! I wouldn't! Not never, mum! (*He feels his face again, tentatively*) Eh, mum, they're getting worser—I'm covered in points and spikes and prickles all over!

Mrs Doasyouwouldbedoneby Look at me, Tom.

He trembles under her steady gaze

Have you been telling lies, Tom?

Tom (*breaking down in tears*) I didn't mean no harm by it, mum! And I didn't eat that many of 'em neither! Just to see what they tasted like. And I promise you I won't never touch nothing that don't belong to me again—only say that you forgive me!

Mrs Doasyouwouldbedoneby Of course I forgive you. Am I not Mrs Doasyouwouldbedoneby? And don't I always forgive everyone the moment they tell me the truth of their own accord?

Tom And will you take away all these nasty spiky prickles?

Mrs Doasyouwouldbedoneby That is a very different matter. You put them there yourself, and only you can take them away.

Tom *How*, mum? Tell me how I am to help myself?

Mrs Doasyouwouldbedoneby By helping others, of course. Have you forgotten where you are going?

Tom To the Other-End-Of-Nowhere.

Mrs Doasyouwouldbedoneby And have you forgotten why you must get there?

Tom Because of Ellie who's lying sick to death in bed, missis—is she no better?

Mrs Doasyouwouldbedoneby (*shaking her head*) No, nor will she be until you have completed your journey—would you like me to bring her here so that you may see her, once, before you go?

Tom If only that were possible!

Mrs Doasyouwouldbedoneby All things are possible—and even though she is lying unconscious in her bed at home, Tom, if she sees you in her dreams, then you may see her too.

Tom But it's not possible, is it missis, that someone as grand as her should dream of me?

Mrs Doasyouwouldbedoneby Haven't I told you once already—all things are possible . . .

She makes a few "magic passes" and the Lights dim again as we hear a few chords of "dreamlike" music

Ellie appears. We might first establish her behind a gauze— in fact, we need to get as close as possible to Kingsley's own description of her arrival: "with long curls floating behind her like a golden cloud, and long robes floating all round her like a silver one"

Tom and Ellie stare hard at each other across the stage with Mrs Doasyou-wouldbedoneby standing between them but in shadow, as:

Tom You *are* here!
Ellie And you're here too—the little chimney-sweep—and you're alive! But are you really real—or is this another dream I'm dreaming? I've dreamed about you so many times before!
Tom Perhaps I'm real but in your dream as well, Ellie.
Ellie (*shaking her head, solemnly*) Dreaming is dreaming; real is real. (*She reaches out across the stage towards him*) And if you *are* real, why can't I touch you?
Tom (*feeling his face*) You wouldn't care to touch me now—I'm all over covered in horrid prickly spikes.
Ellie Perhaps when you get to the Other-End-Of-Nowhere, Tom—the spikes will go.
Tom Do you know about the Other-End-Of-Nowhere too?

During the following reprise, Tom and Ellie move closer to each other—but not close enough to touch

Song 13: The Other-End-Of-Nowhere (Reprise)

(*Singing*) The Other-End-Of-Nowhere, Ellie,
You've heard of it too
Could you come with me
And make this magic dream come true
Ellie I only wish I might but dreams must end
I must go home
And if you are to find it
You must go there on your own

The musical accompaniment carries on through the dialogue

Tom But if I *do* go to the Other-End-Of-Nowhere, I know that I'll find that horrible Mr Grimes and that he'll turn me back into a chimney-sweep again for sure!
Ellie He won't, Tom, no! (*To Mrs Doasyouwouldbedoneby*) Tell him it isn't true.
Mrs Doasyouwouldbedoneby Those that wish to be clean, clean they will be—and those that wish to be foul, foul they will be.
Tom Someone once said that to me before . . .
Mrs Doasyouwouldbedoneby (*to Ellie*) Time to go home.
Tom Don't go, Ellie—please, don't go.
Ellie I must, Tom—I must!

Tom and Ellie move apart from each other again, but still reaching out in an attempt to touch one another, as:

Tom Ellie, come back!

Ellie (*singing*) The Other-End-Of-Nowhere
You must go and I must stay
Although this is a dream
I will remember every day
My every thought goes with you
Just remember that I care
And if you can believe it
You will find it if you dare
The Other-End-Of-Nowhere
The Other-End-Of-Nowhere . . .

Ellie's voice has faded as she herself has disappeared into the darkness—she is now gone completely

Tom Is she gone forever? Have I killed her?

Mrs Doasyouwouldbedoneby Not quite that, Tom—but if you wish to help her, then you must go on to where you do not like to go, and help someone that you like even less.

Tom Is that place the Other-End-Of-Nowhere and is that someone Mr Grimes?

Mrs Doasyouwouldbedoneby Little boys must take the trouble to find out the answers to things themselves, or they will never grow to be men.

Tom Well then, if that is what needs to be done to help Ellie, I am ready to go this minute.

Mrs Doasyouwouldbedoneby That is a brave, good boy—and those were the only words that needed to be said in order for you to complete your journey. God speed, good luck, Tom—and farewell . . .

Scene 5

The Journey

The final part of Tom's journey is accomplished both musically and in an eerie light, suggesting that he is travelling through deep and stormy seas and, possibly, passing strange new fishes and deep-sea creatures

In the professional touring production, a scene was played here in ultra-violet light and with large fish-puppets. Tom entered, wearily, and was attacked by a huge squid. A large fish—which he had befriended in an earlier UV scene—entered and rescued Tom from the squid, finally overpowering it. This scene could be omitted—or producers may wish to attempt it either in this or some other manner

Scene 6

The Other-End-Of-Nowhere

Where, at first and with Tom, all we can see is an iron door. Tom hammers on the door with his fists and the sound echoes off into the gloom. The door squeaks open and Tom finds himself confronted by:

Two stern-looking men with mutton-chop whiskers and dressed in the uniforms of Victorian prison warders

1st Warder Stand up straight and state your business.
Tom If it please you, sir, but could you tell me if this is the Other-End-Of-Nowhere?
2nd Warder What if it is? Do you have to make such a noise about it?
Tom If it is sir, I'd like to come in.
1st Warder Come in? Come in! We never 'as folks as wants to come in 'ere! And them what is in 'ere already is only anxious to get out—not that we ever lets 'em. Name and sentence?
Tom My name is Tom—but I haven't been sentenced to anything, sir—is it a prison then?
2nd Warder Of course it's a prison, laddie—what else might you expect to find at the Other-End-Of-Nowhere, a seaside pier and prom? And if you 'aven't come 'ere to serve a sentence, might one enquire your purpose?
Tom I'm looking for Mr Grimes, the master chimney-sweep.
1st Warder Grimes? 'Im! That blaggard. 'Ee's not entitled to visitors. Why, 'ee's the most unremorseful, hard-hearted, foul-mouthed fellow we've got in charge. What makes you think we'd let you see him?
Tom Mrs Doasyouwouldbedoneby sent me.
2nd Warder Then why didn't you say so in the first place—wasting my time. Come in.

Tom goes through the door which closes slowly behind him

1st Voice (*off*) Visitor for Prisoner Grimes!
2nd Voice (*off*) Visitor for Prisoner Grimes!
3rd Voice (*off*) Pass visitor to chimney number three-five-four!
4th Voice (*off*) Chimney number three-five-four!

We shall hear as many or as few voices as are required and they might also be accompanied by the sound of echoing footsteps along stone-flagged passages

Then as the Light gradually grows, we begin to make out through the gloom a chimney which has Grimes's head and shoulders sticking out of it. In silhouette, beyond Grimes, we can make out a vast array of chimneys stretching off into the distance. Tom and the Warders approach him

1st Warder Attention Mr Grimes! Stand to attention there!
Grimes Attention be blowed. 'Ow can a body stand to attention when 'ee's all jammed up a chimbley and can't so much as twiddle the end of 'is little finger!

At which point, the Warder bangs Grimes over the head with his truncheon

Ow! That 'urt!
2nd Warder It was meant to 'urt, prisoner Grimes. 'ere's a gentleman come to see you.
Grimes Why, Tom! If it ain't Tom!

Tom Hello, Mr Grimes. How are you keeping?

Grimes 'Ow am I keeping? 'Ow am I keeping, you young ragamuffin? 'Ow does it look as if I'm keeping? 'Ow would you keep jammed up all day and all night in a blessed chimbley and not able to do so much as twiddle the end of your little finger?

The Warder wallops Grimes over the head with his truncheon for a second time

Ow-er! To say nothing of being banged over the 'ead reg'lar as clockwork with a great galloping truncheon! I suppose you've come 'ere to laugh at me, you spiteful little street-arab!

Tom No, Mr Grimes—I came to see if I could help you.

Grimes There's nothing I want, excepting beer, and that I can't get—and to smoke just a pipeful of baccy, perhaps, but that I can't get to neither.

Grimes nods down at his pipe which is sticking up out of his breast pocket. Tom reaches to take it out

Tom I'll put your pipe in your mouth for you, Mr Grimes——

But the Warder takes the pipe from Tom, sticks it back in Grimes's pocket and shakes his head, as:

1st Warder It's no good. You'll never manage to light it. His heart's that cold it freezes everything that comes close to him—can't you feel the chill coming out of him now? (*He shivers involuntarily*) Brrr!

Grimes Oh, of course, it's my fauit! Is it any wonder I'm frozen to death—stood standing still in this damp, dark, pestilential prison day after day, week after week, month after month—everything's always *my* fault!

1st Warder And isn't it your fault—or are we to hear more of your excuses? Excuses, excuses, Grimes, always excuses . . .

Song 14: Excuses, Excuses (Reprise)

Warders Excuses, excuses, all the time excuses
Is it your intention to stand idling all the day

Over the next two lines they "beat" him on rhythm with their truncheons

Ex*cuses*, Ex*cuses*, *all* the time ex*cuses*
The *Oth*er-End-Of-*No*where, Grimes,
Is *where* you have to *stay*

Grimes But Mr Warder!
I think you're out of order
I demand respect, sir,
And not your neglect, sir,
There's no beer here
Or even cheese for luncheon

Warders Silence, man, or else you'll get
Another dish of truncheon!

Grimes Owww! Nasty!

Warders No more excuses

No more lazy ruses
Never will you beat a little boy again
Push him up chimbleys
Bully and hurt him—he's
Free while you are locked up
And here you will remain!
We hope it causes aggravation
Not to mention pain!

Over the following dialogue up to Mrs Bedonebyasyoudid's entrance, the theme of "It's A Long Hard Road" is heard unobtrusively

Tom Isn't there anything that I can do to assist you, Mr Grimes? Can't I help you to get out of this chimney?

Grimes shakes his head sadly, as:

2nd Warder Nay, lad. He has come to the place where everybody must help themselves—and the sooner he realizes that, the better.

Grimes Oh yes, of course it's me. Did I ask to be brought here into the prison? Did I ask to be set to sweep your foul chimbleys? Did I ask to have lighted straw put under me to make me clamber up?

And, suddenly, out of the shadows, steps Mrs Bedonebyasyoudid and addresses Grimes sternly:

Mrs Bedonebyasyoudid No! No more did Tom, when you behaved to him in the very same way.

Warders (*leaping to attention*) Ma'am!

Tom Oh, ma'am don't think about me, that's all past and gone, and good times and bad times all pass over. But may I not help poor Mr Grimes? Mayn't I try and get some of these bricks away that he may move his arms?

Mrs Bedonebyasyoudid You may try, of course.

Tom tugs and pulls at the brickwork, but to no avail

Tom It's no good, Mr Grimes—I've come all this way to help you, and now I'm no use at all.

Grimes Nay, lad, you'd best leave me be. You're a kindhearted little lad, and that's the truth—but you'd best be off. It'll start to hail again soon, and that'd beat the eyes out of your head.

Tom How do you know it's going to hail?

Grimes Because it allus rains in this hole—as soon as it's night—hard, driving chunks of hail like pellets of lead.

Mrs Bedonebyasyoudid That hail will never come again, Grimes. I have told you before what that was—your mother's tears, those that she shed when she prayed for you while she was alive—but now the poor woman is dead.

Grimes So . . . So, my old mother's gone then, has she? She was a good-hearted woman, lad, but I treated her bad—ay, and never sent her back so much as a penny-piece after I left. And now it's too late . . . too late! (*He begins to sob, softly at first, but growing in volume*) It's all too late. Go on with thee, thou little man, and don't stand to look at a fellow old enough to be your father that's reduced to tears. I've made my bed and I must lie on it. Foul I would be, and foul I am, as an Irishwoman once told me. It's all too late . . .

Mrs Bedonebyasyoudid It's never too late, Grimes—never too late for a man to regret his past and help himself—and your own tears have washed away the mortar that has held you fast.

Grimes (*wriggling excitedly*) She's right, Tom—by God, she's right! I'm coming loose! Now, lad, you *can* give me a helping hand!

Tom begins to lift down sections of brickwork, perhaps assisted by the Warders as:

Tom It is loose, Mr Grimes, sir—and easy now to shift—it don't even *feel* like bricks any longer—it's like lifting feathers . . .

Mrs Bedonebyasyoudid And shall you obey me in future, Grimes, if I give you this second chance?

Grimes Shall I not! You're stronger than me, and wiser too, and that I know too well. And as for being my own master, I've fared ill enough along that path.

Mrs Bedonebyasyoudid Be it so, then, Grimes—and now you may step out.

Grimes gets down out of the chimney

But remember always: disobey me once, and into a worse place still you go.

Grimes Oh, your ladyship, I'll not do that.

Mrs Bedonebyasyoudid (*to the 1st Warder*) Take him away then.

1st Warder And what am I to do with him, ma'am?

Mrs Bedonebyasyoudid He hasn't *quite* finished his punishment yet. Set him to sweeping out the insides of a couple of dead volcanoes—that should keep him occupied for a year or two—and then, when he is done, I shall review his case again.

Grimes (*as he is led away, apparently overjoyed*) Volcanoes, mum? Oh, bless you, mum! It'll be a pleasure, mum! Thank you, mum! Dead volcanoes! God love you, mum!

Grimes and the Warders exit, Mrs Bedonebyasyoudid turns back to Tom, and:

Mrs Bedonebyasyoudid And now your task is done here, Tom—you can go back to where you came from.

Tom That's easier said than done, ma'am—it took me such a time to get here, shall it take as long to get home again?

Mrs Bedonebyasyoudid Bless the child, of course it won't! For I shall send you back the secret way—up the private back-staircase.

Tom And where might that be, ma'am?

Mrs Bedonebyasyoudid Wherever I say it is, of course. Here, take my hand and close your eyes—and then forget as soon as you have heard them, these magic words:

Oh, backstairs; well-bred backstairs; precious backstairs; commercial backstairs; invaluable backstairs; economical backstairs; requisite backstairs; cosmopolitan backstairs; comfortable backstairs; comprehensive backstairs; accommodating backstairs; reasonable backstairs; aristocratic backstairs; demonstrable backstairs; potent backstairs; all-but-omnipotent backstairs—save us from the consequences of our own actions, and from the cruel fairy, Mrs Bedonebyasyoudid!

As she has recited the "magic words", the music has crept in behind and now the lighting changes into several flashing colours, and then dims—leaving Tom and Mrs Bedonebyasyoudid in a spot as we go to:

Scene 7

Back On Dry Land

Where the four-poster bed has again been trucked on but is, for the moment, invisible in the darkness

Mrs Bedonebyasyoudid Now you are safely up the stairs and home again and all is well.

Tom (*opening his eyes*) But what about Ellie, ma'am?

Mrs Bedonebyasyoudid Heaven's sakes, child, when I say that all is well I mean all is well! I don't go in for half-measures!

The lighting grows and now we can see the four-poster with the group consisting of Sir John; the Doctor; the Housemaid; the Nurse and the Gamekeeper standing in frozen attitudes around it. They remain "frozen" as Ellie gets up off the bed and runs across to join Tom. Mrs Bedonebyasyoudid moves back into shadow. Tom and Ellie take hold of each other's hands and gaze into each other's face

Tom Ellie—oh, Ellie! You *are* quite better—you are quite well!

Ellie And Tom—oh, Tom—it *isn't* a dream any longer—you're safe and real! (*Embracing him*) And not prickly and spiky any longer!

Mrs Bedonebyasyoudid Enough of that! Attention, both of you—now look at me, and tell me who I am.

Tom You're Mrs Bedonebyasyoudid.

But as she moves out of the shadows we see that she has turned into:

Ellie You're Mrs Doasyouwouldbedoneby!

And now she removes her half-mask and we see that she has now become:

Tom Ecky Moses! You're the Irishwoman I met on the day I went to Harthover.

Irishwoman I am all of them and I am none of them, as you will one day learn—but not yet, young things, not yet. You have your lives before you.

Tom And shall we marry and be happy ever after?

Irishwoman My dear child, what a foolish notion! Don't you know that no-one ever marries in a fairy-tale under the rank of a prince or princess . . . ?

She takes their hands, one each side of her, and the following number starts half-spoken:

Song 15: Finale

But you'll certainly both be incredibly
Happy throughout your lives
Ellie is well and my brave little chap
He's come back from the deep to survive

She moves across to the bed and, as she names each character, they "unfreeze" and move down to join, embrace—or whatever, depending upon their household status—Tom and Ellie

The Doctor, the Nurse, the Gamekeeper, Sir John
And finally Grimes—who knows he did wrong.

Oh, they've never been, ever been,
Quite so happy in all their lives

Company Here at Harthover Hall, we pray
That you too have been happy
And enjoyed our play
All assembled wish you happiness
And we thank you all for being
Such kind guests
So good's triumphed over evil
Right over wrong
Celebrate now, let's all sing along
For we've never been, ever been,
Quite so happy in the days and months and years
Of our natural lives

Over the above, the Housemaid brings on a tray containing glasses of wine which are handed round and the cast toast themselves and the audience as—

the CURTAIN *falls*

FURNITURE AND PROPERTY LIST

ACT I

Scene 1

On stage: Table. *On it:* tankard for **Grimes**
Bench
Inn-sign

Off stage: Tankard of ale **(Potman)**
Hand-cart full of brushes and equipment **(Tom)**
Tankard of ale, bread-and-cheese in handkerchief **(Potman)**

Personal: **Grimes:** pipe, spotted handkerchief

Scene 2

On stage: Low dry-stone wall
Milestone

Off stage: Hand-cart with brushes etc. **(Tom)**

Personal: **Grimes:** handkerchief with bread-and-cheese
Irishwoman: bundle of belongings
Tom: 3 marbles, button with bit of string in pocket

Scene 3

On stage: Piece of garden statuary, or length of formal decorative wall, or flower-decked gothic urn

Off stage: Hand-cart with brushes etc. **(Tom)**

Personal: **Gamekeeper:** game-bag containing gin-trap

Scene 4

On stage: Ornate fireplace. *On mantelpiece*: ornament
Couple of pieces of furniture covered with dust-sheets

Off stage: Sacking, brushes, weights **(Tom)**

Personal: **Grimes:** bottle of drink in pocket

Scene 5

On stage: Window
Fireplace. *Above it:* picture. *In hearth:* fire-irons
Four-poster bed with bedding

Cheval mirror
Wash-stand. *On it:* wash-bowl, water-jug, face flannel, soap, etc.

Off stage: Lighted lanterns **(Sir John, Housemaid, Gamekeeper, Nurse,** etc.**)**—optional

SCENE 6

On stage: Rocking-chair
Book for **Old Woman**
Stool. *On it:* jug of milk, cup, plate with bread
Outhouse. *In it:* hay on floor
Fence

Off stage: Pile of **Tom**'s clothing with 3 marbles and button with string in pocket **(Gardener)**

SCENE 7

On stage: Gravestone
Willow-tree
Flowers for **Ellie**

SCENE 8

On stage: Water-reeds
Boulders

Off stage: Puppet fishes (**Stage Management**)—optional

ACT II

SCENE 1

On stage: As Scene 8

Off stage: Puppet Water Babies **(Stage Management)**—optional

SCENE 2

On stage: Sand effect on sea-bed

SCENE 3

On stage: **Ellie**'s 4-poster bed with bedding (on truck)
Lighted oil-lamp for **Housemaid**
Stethoscope for **Doctor**

SCENE 4

On stage: Lobster-pot
Rock/cupboard. *In it:* jars of sweets etc.

Off stage: Puppet Water Babies **(Stage Management)**—optional

Personal: **Mrs Bedonebyasyoudid:** birch-cane, half-mask, spectacles (required throughout), jar of sweets
Mrs Doasyouwouldbedoneby: half-mask (required throughout)

SCENE 5

On stage: Puppet fish and sea-creatures—optional

SCENE 6

On stage: Iron door
Chimneys

Personal: **Warders:** truncheons
Grimes: pipe

SCENE 7

On stage: 4-poster bed on truck

Off stage: Tray with glasses of wine **(Housemaid)**

Personal: **Mrs Bedonebyasyoudid:** Mrs Doasyouwouldbedoneby's half-mask (to swap with her own on page 47)

LIGHTING PLOT

Property fittings required: several lighted lanterns (optional), UV lighting (optional), lighted oil-lamp

Various simple interior and exterior settings

ACT I, Scene 1

To open: Bright general lighting

Cue 1 **Grimes** and **Tom** move on (Page 3)
Fade lights

ACT I, Scene 2

To open: Sunny exterior lighting

Cue 2 **Grimes:** "... finished with you yet either——" (Page 7)
Fade sun effect

Cue 3 **Tom** and **Grimes** head off (Page 8)
Fade lights

ACT I, Scene 3

To open: General exterior lighting

Cue 4 **Housemaid** escorts **Tom** and **Grimes** towards house (Page 11)
Fade lights

ACT I, Scene 4

To open: General interior lighting

Cue 5 **Grimes:** "... when I do lay hold of him ..." (Page 14)
Black-out

ACT I, Scene 5

To open: Interior lighting

Cue 6 **Tom** makes his exit (Page 16)
Dim lights; optional—increase lighting downstage as figures enter carrying lighted lanterns

Cue 7 During choreographed chase (Page 16)
Increase lighting

Cue 8 During final chorus of Song 4 (Page 17)
Begin to fade lights

ACT I, SCENE 6

To open: General exterior lighting—morning sun

Cue 9 **Sir John:** "The poor lad's gone then." (Page 21)
Pause, then fade morning sunlight into shadow

Cue 10 **Housemaid** and **Nurse** enter and join the others (Page 22)
Fade to black-out

ACT I, SCENE 7

To open: General exterior lighting

Cue 11 **Irishwoman:** ". . . turned into Water Babies." (Page 23)
Dim lights; bring up UV lighting (if used)

ACT I, SCENE 8

To open: Optional UV lighting; underwater effect

Cue 12 **Tom** enters (Page 24)
Replace UV lighting (if used) with general underwater lighting

ACT II, SCENE 1

To open: As end Scene 8

Cue 13 As **Irishwoman** sings (Page 26)
UV lighting (if used) for puppets

Cue 14 **Water Babies** swim off (Page 27)
Change from UV lighting (if used) to general state

Cue 15 **Tom:** ". . . some way—somehow . . ." (Page 27)
Dim lighting

Cue 16 **Male Water-Otter:** "Listen!" (Page 29)
Dim lighting further

Cue 17 **All:** "Louder the river runs!" (Page 29)
Dim lighting still further, leaving UVs (if used) as predominant source

Cue 18 **Company** (*singing*): ". . . when will the storm be past?" (Page 30)
Lightning

Cue 19 **Company** (*singing*): "Look out for the lightning flash" (Page 30)
Lightning

Cue 20 **Company** (*singing*): "Quickly, safely, down to the sea" (Page 30)
Warm overhead light of the sun overtakes darkness and UVs (if used)

ACT II, SCENE 2

To open: Blue underwater lighting

Cue 21 **Tom** closes his eyes once more and concentrates (Page 32)
Dim lights

ACT II, SCENE 3

To open: Pool of light on Ellie's bed—from oil-lamp

Cue 22 **Doctor:** "... indeed one might ..." (Page 33)
Dim lights as bed is trucked off; bring up spot on **Tom**

ACT II, SCENE 4

To open: Underwater lighting

Cue 23 **Mrs Bedonebyasyoudid:** "... straightaway off to sleep ..." (Page 38)
Dim lights

Cue 24 **Mrs Bedonebyasyoudid:** "... they are coming now ..." (Page 38)
UV lighting (if used), covered in a "special" or follow spot downstage

Cue 25 **Water Babies** swim off, giggling happily at their success (Page 38)
Change from UV lighting (if used) to general state

Cue 26 **Mrs Doasyouwouldbedoneby** makes a few "magic passes" (Page 40)
Dim lights

ACT II, SCENE 5

To open: Eerie underwater lighting with optional UV lighting

No cues

ACT II, SCENE 6

To open: Gloomy lighting

Cue 27 As Voices call out (Page 43)
Gradually increase lighting; silhouette effect of vast array of chimneys stretching off into distance

Cue 28 **Mrs Bedonebyasyoudid:** "... from the cruel fairy, Mrs Bedonebyasyoudid!" (Page 47)
Change lighting to several flashing colours, then dim, leaving **Tom** *and* **Mrs Bedonebyasyoudid** *in spot*

ACT II, SCENE 7

To open: Spot on **Tom** and **Mrs Bedonebyasyoudid**

Cue 29 **Mrs Bedonebyasyoudid:** "... for half-measures!" (Page 47)
Increase lighting

EFFECTS PLOT

ACT I

Cue 1	**Grimes:** "... finished with you yet either——" *Chill wind blows up*	(Page 7)
Cue 2	**Grimes:** "... afraid of you! I'm not!" *Increase wind*	(Page 7)
Cue 3	**Grimes** and **Tom** head off *Fade wind*	(Page 8)
Cue 4	**Irishwoman** moves back into the darkness; **Tom** is left alone *Church-bells far away in distance—fade after a few moments*	(Page 18)
Cue 5	**Sir John:** "The poor lad's gone then." *Sonorous tolling of church-bells close at hand*	(Page 21)
Cue 6	When ready for Scene 7 *Fade church-bells*	(Page 22)

ACT II

Cue 7	**Male Water-Otter:** "Listen!" *Plip-plop of raindrops on surface of water*	(Page 29)
Cue 8	**Company** (*singing*): "We must all swim down to the sea" *Thunder*	(Page 30)
Cue 9	**Company** (*singing*): "Quickly, safely, down to the sea" *Thunder*	(Page 30)
Cue 10	**Tom** hammers on iron door *Echo knocks*	(Page 43)
Cue 11	(*optional*) As **Tom** and **Warders** go through door *Echoing footsteps along stone-flagged passages*	(Page 43)

MADE AND PRINTED IN GREAT BRITAIN BY
LATIMER TREND & COMPANY LTD PLYMOUTH
MADE IN ENGLAND